In Deep With You

SHANDRA WARD

Literary Freedom Publishing, LLC

Visit our website:
www.literaryfreedompub.com
In Deep With You
Copyright © 2023 by Literary Freedom Publishing, LLC.
All Rights Reserved.

No part of this publication may be reproduced, stored or transmitted in any form or by any means, electronic, mechanical, photocopying, recording, scanning, or otherwise without written permission from the publisher. It is illegal to copy this book, post it to a website, or distribute it by any other means without permission.

This novel is entirely a work of fiction. The names, characters and incidents portrayed in it are the work of the author's imagination. Any resemblance to actual persons, living or dead, events or localities is entirely coincidental.

Cover Design by Literary Freedom Publishing, LLC.

Shandra Ward asserts the moral right to be identified as the author of this work.

Designations used by companies to distinguish their products are often claimed as trademarks. All brand names and product names used in this book and on its cover are trade names, service marks, trademarks, and registered trademarks of their respective owners. The publishers and the book are not associated with any product or vendor mentioned in this book. None of the companies referenced within the book have endorsed the book.

Printed in the United States of America.

First Printing: September 2023

Literary Freedom Publishing, LLC.

Contents

The Night She Was Stolen	1
Surviving Daytona	9
Empty Birthdays	25
Waves	39
Hidden Flames	53
Old Faces, Old Wounds	65
Under Fire	79
Heatwave	95
Erotic Propositions	103
The Other Side of a Coin	119
Smoke	129
Black Russian Roulette	149
Home Is Where the Heart Has Always Been	165
Meet the Author	175

The Night She Was Stolen

"To steal the dance out of the soul of a woman, that makes you a monster. But to plant a sweet song in her heart that can heal her, you must be a King..."

The jazzy sounds of John Coltrane blowing a horn should've been an insignificant sound for any eighteen-year-old girl to hear that was in Astrid Montgomery's position. But for her, it was the one sound she held onto that reminded her she wasn't dead.

"I swear, this is my last time doing this. After tonight, lose my damn number."

"You plan on takin' this money or not?"

The words seemed to float in and out of time for Astrid. She was unsure of how she got back to her room on the Swanny Merriott Ship. She was very sure of everything before then. She was standing out on the ship's deck confessing her feelings to her best friend Donovan Price. She rehearsed everything beforehand. What she would say. How she would say it. Had in her mind that she'd be leaving soon because she was, and by then it was too late.

Within the next two months, Astrid and Donovan would graduate alongside twenty-five other seniors from Camden High. And afterwards, she would be on her way to Harvard University to study dance - ballet to be specific, and every other thing out of the ordinary for a caramel skinned black girl coming out of the streets of Saxton. But before that happened, she needed to take a bold step and confess something she knew since the day she met Donovan in grade school English class.

She loved him.

Her confession did not go as planned though.

Astrid told Donovan that she loved him, and he rejected her. And his best friend Zane Keys was to blame. Unexpectedly, Donovan's words came out harsh. So harsh that it created a wound on the inside of Astrid's chest, and she dismissed herself before the shame could settle too far down on the inside of her.

"*Why would you put me in this position?*" Donovan inquired of her abrasively. "*It's not like I haven't thought about it. I admit it. We've gone over this before three summers ago down at the Polo game arcade. I know my response was different then, so that's on me. But Z, well, that day, he kind of put everything in perspective for me...*"

"*Z?*" Astrid responded in confusion. "*Perspective?*" *Those were the only words she could form.*

"*Yeah, you get it? Two best friends going together? It ain't my style. Honestly, we wouldn't make a good couple, anyway. I like the type of girls I like. And you...man...you get where I'm going Astrid?*"

The words left Astrid dumbfounded. Three summers ago, she was bold enough to kiss Donovan, and he returned the favor back. Neither of them ever discussed it. Astrid figured fear had its hold on Donovan, so she waited until this very night. The night of their senior trip out on the Swanny Merriott. She was quickly convinced, though. She may as well have kept silent all together.

Just what the hell did Zane know about her or what type of girlfriend she could be to Donovan? Astrid figured the same thing he thought he knew when he talked Jarold Dixon, one of the front liners on the Camden High football team, out of taking her to the

Sophomore dance just a year ago. The same thing he thought when he talked Keagan Williams into breaking up with her on her fifteenth birthday.

Astrid didn't bother asking Donovan what he meant by her not being the type of girl he went out with. She already knew. At eighteen, she was sure she was the only girl growing up on the rough side of Saxton who was still a virgin. It was a flaw her sisters never let her live down. But to have it thrown in her face by her own best friend, Astrid felt burned.

On the wings of emotion, she dismissed herself to find a place on the ship that she wasn't permitted and would be disciplined at the hands of on-board school staff, the Parakeet bar.

There, Astrid met a man named Othello whose skin was as light as the desert sand in Dubai. She knew that the possibility of Othello being his real name was more than likely a fluke, but having the attention of the opposite sex, a grown man at that—it felt sweeter than the cords on a blues record at that moment.

Astrid and Othello talked long enough to become well acquainted. The beautiful man caressed her with entertaining words and bought her a drink that made her insides feel so good she no longer felt the weight of rejection or her anger at the likes of Zane.

Still, even while under the influence, the voice of common sense rang loud to her.

Go back to your damn room, Astrid. You'll get over Donovan. No boy is worth getting drunk and suffering getting expelled for. You have far too much at stake.

The words were sharp and clear. Anita Baker voice crooning from the speakers inside the Parakeet Bar didn't stand a chance against the voice scolding Astrid on the inside.

Go back to your room, Astrid, it said. *The cruise will be over soon. You and Donovan will still be close. The only real reason you're angry is because you're still a virgin.*

Laying on the bed inside of her cabin, Astrid wished she listened to the voice of warning as she overheard the voices from across the room. The motion of the Swanny ship made her body feel as though she were floating. But it was the crooning of John Coltrane's horn sweeping through the cracked window from the senior party on the bottom deck that seemed to cradle her like a newborn.

"I can't believe I'm doing this shit," a familiar voice stressed to Othello. The voice was heavy with regret; haunting. "Fuckin' brother would kill me."

"You wanna start this late in the game by giving a fuck just because you know her? Should I remind you that you're the one who led me to her? You're the one who decided to go through with the job given to you by—"

"Look, just make this shit quick."

"I'm paying you my money. I suggest you give me the time that I deserve. Or we can cut ties on this all together..."

There was silence in the cabin for a short moment, and then the clicking sound of the air vent kicking on disturbed the peace. With a groan from her lips, Astrid used all the strength she could to maneuver her head toward the voices. She took in two figures, but her eyes settled on the one most familiar, Othello's.

What's happening? Astrid thought.

Where's,,,Donovan? Where's...Lisa? Where's...Carmen? Why can't I move? How did I get here?

Astrid's mind became so barricaded with the whereabouts of everyone who was aboard the ship that she considered a trustworthy contact for what was supposed to be a three-day cruise to celebrate the last year achievements of the Camden High Seniors. Then the real question formed, what was Othello doing in her cabin?

How did he know where she rested?

In all the alcohol consumption she allowed herself to get carried away with, revealing her room number was never brought into the mix.

She told him she would be okay getting back, that she didn't need the comfort. Othello attempted to oblige her anyway, and Astrid shoved him away before falling face first to the wooden deck floor beneath her. Anita Baker's voice faded out, and another genre of music spilled in.

Damn annoying ass salsa music, Astrid thought. And then...black.

When Astrid attempted to move her limbs with the little ability she had, she realized her movement was restricted. Both of her arms were roped off and bound to the bed.

"Just do your best and try not to be so damn rough." The supposed voice of reason said to Othello. "I need her in one piece unlike your previous works."

Othello blew the sideman off. "Yeah, whateva'."

Astrid groaned from the shooting pain writhing through her brain. Her heart beat furiously. She was hot all over, as if a fire was burning her from the inside out. She kept her eyes on the two figures. Aside from the man from the bar, the other moved in a way that was all too familiar. She couldn't place her finger on who he was. Both of them—their faces were covered in black ski masks to match their dark wardrobe. It was the aroma of Othello that gave him away. Astrid could still smell the apple pie margarita she wasted on him in between conversations. The clumsy move embarrassed the hell out of her, but Othello put Astrid's mind at ease by playing it off and buying her another one.

"Plea–please..." Astrid attempted to speak. "Let me..." Her words seemed to get stuck at the exit of her lips and she became far too lazy to get up the nerve to say more.

The two figures looked over at her for a second. "How much did you give her?" the figure to the left asked.

"Enough," Othello replied carelessly.

He walked over to the foot of the bed to stare down at a mildly conscious Astrid. Reaching out, he trailed a finger along the opening flap of her v-neck shirt all the way down to the open entrance of her skirt. He roamed at a spot between her thighs, and then, roughly, he gripped them and parted them open.

The pain registered through Astrid's body like a rocket of fire. *Please, stop!* She thought. *Please! Don't! I've never had...*

She took in the tattoo of five skulls on Othello's left hand.

"You mind excusing us," Othello said to his partner.

Astrid looked at the other stranger with pleading eyes, desperate and full of sorrow. For a moment, the person locked in on her as if he were thinking about his actions, as if he wanted to recant everything that was about to unravel. But just as swiftly, he dropped his head and walked out of the room leaving the door to clasp shut behind him.

If Astrid could scream the moment Othello dropped his pants, ripped through her panties, and entered her, she was sure the sea and all its secrets would have heard her. There was the sound of the ship making its traditional quaking churn mingling over Mr. Coltrane, and Astrid took it as the ship screaming for her instead.

For what seemed like forever, the man above her pumped in and out of her with no mercy as if he were trying to reach inside and kill whatever dreams she had. When he was done, he stared down at her barely breathing as he pulled back up his pants.

"You're not a virgin anymore beautiful Astrid," he muttered in a twisted tone.

A tear slipped down the corners of Astrid's eyes and soaked down into the veil of her hair on the pillow as the man exited. He'd left her to die there, and she was sure she would.

But it was the person who came knocking on her door that wouldn't let that happen.

"Astrid!" they called out from the outside of her cabin door. "Yo, Astrid! It's me! Open up!"

With everything inside of her, Astrid wanted to talk back but she couldn't. It was as if her voice was swallowed up. She groaned and shut her eyes.

Just let me die, she thought. *Please, just let me die.*

"Yo, Astrid!" The voice called out to her again. "Come on! I know you're mad at me about Donovan, but you gotta let me explain! I have something I need to say to you!"

The pounding came once more, and Astrid winced at the rhythmic pain from her head and between her legs that seemed to coincide with one another. There was the sound of the doorknob being fondled with and the room door parting open. When the person stepped in, the sound of a sharp gasp echoed around the cabin. It was followed by a slew of curse words. Cold air followed in like a ghost and wrapped itself around Astrid's naked body.

"Astrid..." the person said in a grieved tone. "What the fuck..."

She felt a large arm slide underneath the weight of her body as they pulled her into their embrace. The swift aroma of a familiar cologne caressed her nostrils.

"Astrid," they called to her. "Wake up, baby. Come on, wake up. This is not how I wanted this to turn out."

They shook her body violently enough for her to part her eyes open a little. Astrid blinked a few times at the blurring face hovering over her before it came clearly into view. She stared up into a pair of beautiful hickory brown eyes.

Zane? She thought.

"Who did this to you?" he demanded angrily; his eyes shadowed painfully with tears. "Tell me! I'll kill that motherfucka' myself! You know I got people!"

With the little strength she had, Astrid frowned. She tried to talk, but once again, her tongue was paralyzed. If she could have spoken, she would've asked him, *Since when did you ever give a fuck about me? You talked Donavan into rejecting me just like you did Jarold and Keagan!*

Fuck you, Zane!

Fuck Donovan!

Fuck Othello and every other man from this day forward!

The most Astrid could do was stare up into Zane's eyes as he held her. He was holding her as if she were some glass figurine. Of all the times the two expressed their disdain for each other throughout the years until hate lay dormant between them, Astrid was sure she was seeing things. This guy resembled nothing about the traditional cocky, egotistical, heartless, suave dope boy she knew as Zane Keys. This Zane staring down at her had eyes that were delicate and swelled with both anger and tears at the condition of her. He mirrored someone who cared.

"Who did this?" Zane asked again in a burdened voice. "Who hurt you?"

Astrid wanted to answer, but unconsciousness was calling her with a vengeance, and she couldn't run away. The last words she heard were, "I'm so sorry. I should've been bold enough to finally tell you the truth..."

Zane's words were followed with a gentle brush of his lips along Astrid's cheek.

Surviving Daytona
ASTRID

12 years later

Astrid Montgomery could always see the same ghost of every man she ever loved in her lover Daytona's eyes, but the most obvious and prevalent one was Othello's.
It was indecisive.
Full of malice.
Full of noise.
Contradicting.
Predictable.
Controlling a leech.
It knew nothing about what it wanted from Astrid, most of the time, except to strip her of the little dignity she had left. But whenever it set out to have its untimely set motive, the drive was strong. Its desire was to wound her deeper than she already was. Some would say Astrid was crazy for seeing such things. Her older sisters, Sky and Trina, to name a couple. But they, along with most people, weren't aware of the burden of grudges and unforgiveness. Sky and Trina knew nothing about being taken against their will with no way out.

Not like Astrid did. They knew nothing about being so devastated by life that it made one angry and bitter to the point of poisoning one's own selves.

That's what she was.

Astrid was angry, bitter, and for good reason. But most of all, out of all these things, Astrid was dying.

"Astrid," Serenity called to her from the opposite end of the cordless phone. "Are you there?"

Astrid, laying on her side with her cheek pressed to the carpeted floor of her bedroom closet, softly cleared her throat. "Yes..." she replied weakly. She kept her eyes closed for the time being. The pain attached to her womb seemed to be easier to bear that way. It was also a much easier way to block out the noise seeping in from the outside.

"I have a place for you and Ariyah here in Saxton. If you would like, I can come get you..."

Astrid took a deep breath. "I...I can't leave right now."

"I think you can," Serenity refuted gently. "And you want to. You call me every time you're in this space."

"Don't remind me."

Serenity Ashford-Rushmoore, wife to one of Saxton City's savviest businessmen, Blaze Rushmoore, had a tone like velvet. It was the softest voice Astrid ever encountered, and she didn't know why she gravitated to it. She didn't like soft things. She wasn't a soft person. Not the way she used to be. If she were a lesbian, she figured it would make sense that she would be stricken, but she was never plagued with that type of curiosity. Having the profession of some Hollywood director who's obsessed with voice overs for commercials or cartoons, that would be understandable too. But Astrid hated cartoons, and as far as she was concerned, commercials were merely leverage for well needed bathroom breaks.

"All you have to do is tell me where you are..." Serenity said.

Astrid claimed silence for a short while as the searing pain went rocketing through her body again. "Emm..." she groaned.

"Astrid Montgomery, I owe you. Please, let me help."

"We're...all the way...in Daytona, Florida."

Serenity grunted slightly humored at the reminder. "I'm aware of that, love."

"That's five hours away. Too damn far."

"Not for me or my husband."

"Emm."

"Let's see. By car, I can be to you by three in the morning. But if we're talking helicopter, I can get to you in three hours less than that."

Astrid grunted. "My man's name ain't named after the city we live in for play, Mrs. Rushmoore."

"And my husband's name isn't Blaze by chance, Ms. Montgomery. Saxton is as much of your home as it is mine. You should know."

"I left for a reason."

"Yes, and now you have a reason to come back."

A strained, but thoughtful smile kissed Astrid's lips. She had no business talking to the woman she blamed at one point for being responsible for her sister's death. Those weren't necessarily her feelings anymore, but they had been. Serenity, who was relentless in speaking with her after the real murderers of Blu were caught. Phone call after phone call for the last five years, Serenity sought caringly about Astrid's state of being. As if she gave a damn. As if somehow seeing about Astrid would grant her a golden ticket only she didn't come off as an opportunist. It took two years into the five for Astrid to give in. The reason being...she had no one.

"Astrid..." Serenity tugged at her once more.

Astrid hugged herself even tighter. "Can I give you my answer tomorrow morning?" She mumbled.

"Okay. Tomorrow morning, then." Serenity accepted.

Astrid pressed the call end button and let the phone slip from her ear and down onto the carpet with a soft thunk. She continued to lay there in the closet with her eyes closed, but aside from the slow vocal crooning of Keith Sweat blaring, it was also the constant racket from the main living room that triggered her to open her eyes again.

Through the partial opening of the double door closet, Astrid peered through the crack of the bedroom door. It gave her a free view into the living room where her lover, Daytona, and three of his men, Kilo, Free, and Levi were occupied with their traditional game of spades. The men chugged their usual brown liquor like a batch of black pirates while cursing and exchanging belly filled laughs. But no matter how much noise they made, Astrid could not block out the cries of her twelve-month-old daughter, Ariyah. Daytona had turned up the music to drown her out, but Keith Sweat was no match for the cries of their baby girl.

Usually, Astrid would go over into the next room and comfort Ariyah the way a mother should. She hated the ruckus of Daytona and his men just as much, but her body wouldn't let her move. At times, Ariyah seemed smart enough to know these things, and, eventually, she'd stop crying. As if she knew her mother not showing up to coddle her meant the monster in her womb was holding her captive. And then, there were other times like that very moment where Ariyah would cry to the top of her lungs as if she demanded Astrid snap out of the torment and come see about her.

Give mama a moment, Ari, Astrid thought. *It'll pass. I promise. Just hold on...*

"That's another hit for me!" Daytona carried on. Like a runner up on some five-star game show, he shot up to his feet and tossed his winning set down on the table. He scored lucky in the game of spades for the fourth time in a row.

"Nah, brotha," Kilo protested. He was a slender man with extremely protruding veins that seemed to only come out when he was furious and Daytona taking all of his wife's bill money was a good enough reason to act a fool. "You cheatin'. Since when the hell you been this good at spades?"

"Since ya mama taught me how to play," Daytona fired back.

Free laughed from a deep place inside of him. It was from the same place he stored his bitterness when Kilo took his stash in the last game. "Settle your ass down, Lo." He told him.

"Daytona's having a lucky ass night. You had it last weekend. Or did you forget?"

"Fuck that!" Kilo banged his hand on the table.

"Yeah, alright salty ass nigga!" Daytona told him in an edgy tone.

"Chill, Lo." Levi said. "Just tell your main broad you had to spend your Benjamin's on something important. Like your damn pride!"

All of them excluding Kilo continued to be swept away with humor at him being a sore loser. "Yeah?" Kilo nodded bitterly. "Why don't I take my ass in the damn room and tell Astrid how you gambled away her diamond earrings you bought her last year…"

Daytona grunted and peered over in the direction of the bedroom as though he could feel Astrid's eyes on him before smirking. "I ain't fucked up 'bout her," he spat as he took a lazy sip from his bottle. "I ain't fucked up 'bout her one damn bit. And I suggest you sit your ass down spewing out threats in my place."

"My damn woman would be raisin' hell hearin' me say some shit like that," Free said.

"Sounds to me like you need to get a more submissive bitch," Daytona retorted.

It wasn't out of the ordinary for a man of Daytona's caliber to be so vulgar. And like always, Free didn't hold back on laying into his ass. Mostly because they were actually blood.

"How many times have I told you, her name is not bitch," Free corrected with disdain. "And for the record, if you feel like that about yo ole lady then maybe you need to ditch her ass."

"Nah, he won't do that," Kilo interjected. "Too much freedom to give up."

Daytona took a sip of his liquor and burped. "Damn right," he bragged. "I got a submissive bitch."

Yes.

Othello was very much present. Astrid could see it.

She could feel him.

Last night, it was Henry Wilks—the broker from two years ago. He didn't last long. He wasn't a man who dared to drink or smoke. He wouldn't dare sabotage his system like that. But the lies he stitched together like precious quilts—as though he would win some golden prize was crudely phenomenal.

Last night, Daytona did that.

He strolled through the door smelling of flowery perfume so strong it stung Astrid's nostrils into a night full of aching sneezes. It was to the point of her not being able to fully enjoy the movie Juice she was so peacefully watching beforehand. She remembered verbatim what her last thought was before all hell broke loose on the inside of her. Before that voice of warning came and scolded her for not leaving for the hundred time. It was what she always thought whenever Omar Epps' character, Quincy, came on the screen.

That's a bad ass lil hip hop kid, referring to the scene of him battling it out in a record spinning contest with a random opponent.

Astrid confronted Daytona about his obvious misdeeds the moment her suspicions were triggered. And just like Henry, Daytona reached into the deepest parts of himself and pulled out the biggest lie he could find.

Astrid didn't argue.

She feared setting off the pain inside of her. Not to mention the voice on the inside of her warned her not to.

There's nothing else to do but leave, the internal voice spoke to her. *Get your baby and go. Before it's too late. Go.*

Astrid held her hand over her stomach as the pain went shooting through her like a firecracker. It radiated through her entire body. The pain cradled her all day. From the rising of the sun overshadowing Daytona City to the current moment while the moon was full. It hurt so much that Astrid called out from her job for the second time in the week.

"You plan on gettin' that rich ass thug you have to pay your way? Cause at the rate you goin', your ass going to be out of a job..." Mrs. Baxter, her boss, remarked before slamming the receiver down in her ear.

Astrid was in too much pain to even argue back. It was the longest she'd ever been riddled with her ailment. As if her body was finally growing tired and was telling her to go crawl in a corner and die there. If she did, she knew Daytona wouldn't give a damn. He didn't give a damn about much if it wasn't getting money, drugs and random loose women. Some nights she was his loose woman, and not by choice.

Closing her eyes back, Astrid balled her hands into the carpet.

"God, if you want me to die..." She cried to herself. "Just take me already."

Astrid didn't believe much in anything outside of what she saw. At least not until the night of Othello. That night, she was sure he followed her everywhere and the only thing that seemed to make him disappear out of her dreams was God when she got scared enough to call on him. At times though, she was convinced even God had it out for her too.

Eventually, sleep claimed Astrid and for the next two hours she was peaceful again until she heard the creaking of the closet doors being snatched open. She grimaced at the invasion.

"Get your ass up," Daytona barked at her.

She heard his voice before opening her eyes and looking up at his muscular, tall shadow. He reached up and pulled at the long string attached to the closet light, turning it on. Like a pair of unwanted headlights, it beamed down on Astrid, and she shielded her hand over her eyes.

"So, your ass has been on the phone again?" Daytona spat.

"That's what you startin' to do now while you swear your ass is in pain?"

"Leave me alone, Day." Astrid groaned.

He reached down to grab the phone off the floor. "I'm not doing shit. Fuck was you talkin' to this time?"

"None of your business."

"Bull. I know you've been plottin' with one of your bitches? And just where the hell do you plan on going?" Daytona questioned with disdain.

"You don't need to know all of that?" Astrid mumbled. She grew the nerve to tell him that she was leaving him a year ago. The problem was, she never acted. But somehow, Daytona would take her threat seriously every time. Astrid reasoned that it was because he knew that eventually, one day, her threat would turn serious. And he had no problem reminding her what would happen if she tried.

"Woman, don't you dare get smart with me?" Daytona raved on. "We both know that shit won't end well for you."

Dropping her hand, Astrid rolled over on her back. Her actions weren't out of the norm. There were plenty of times where she ached to the point of lying on the floor and balling herself up there. Being in the closet was simply another way for her not to feel foolish; weak. Daytona wouldn't dare lift a finger to comfort her. He wouldn't dare do anything except stare, and claim every other hour about how sad it was that as a black woman Astrid couldn't find a doctor good enough to put a stop to her ailments. Believe it or not, those were the good days because no blows were thrown. Not in the physical sense.

Astrid sucked in a rugged breath and closed her eyes again for a moment. She wished she were something close to a sea creature. A fucking mermaid perhaps. Maybe a goddamn whale. If she were, she would float so far out into the currents until no one could find her.

"Don't make me repeat myself," Daytona warned her before walking over to the bed and claiming a spot on the edge of it. He reeked of alcohol, and it trailed.

After another short moment, Astrid reached out for balance on the hold of the closet wall and tugged herself up to her knees, and then her feet. She breathed heavily, the corners of her eyes burning with tears. "You're free to repeat whatever you damn well please," she told Daytona.

The difference between Astrid and most battered women; she wasn't afraid as much. Coming to blows with Daytona always ended with him having the upper hand, of course. But she never backed down.

"I swear, your mouth will be the death of you when it comes to me." Daytona emphasized.

"Is that a promise?"

Daytona eyed her. "You got all of this mouth for me, but you couldn't tell that nigga to pull out of you that night?"

The words pierced her like flaming daggers. It wasn't the first time he said it but of all the insults Astrid could take, some of them stung her to silence.

Never tell a nigga about your past heartbreaks. He'll just use it against you, Astrid recalled her sister, Blu's words.

"Yeah," Daytona spat as he stood again. "I thought that might shut you up. So, you gon tell me who you were on the phone with, or do I need to press redial?" He continued to badger. "Or maybe I need to remind you which one of us has the upper hand."

Astrid's eyes fell to Daytona's hands. He'd dropped the phone on the bed to ball them up into fists half the size of hers. She surveyed the room in which she stood. It was beautiful in a hoodrich sort of way, and full of pricey and exotic things.

Her bed was Queen sized but she didn't feel like she was a Queen at all. The floor was a carpeted blush pink. A giant vintage picture of Pam Grier as foxy brown hung up on the far wall and another of Angela Davis on the opposite end. A marble lamp set on a long blush pink marble dresser covered in jewelry boxes and make up bags.

Astrid's eyes landed on the golden vase down at the end of the dresser.

"I don't want to fight with you," she told Daytona as she looked back at him.

Daytona took a step toward her. "Then I suggest your ass start talkin'."

Astrid parted her lips to fire off, but the erupting sounds of baby Ariyah's cries paused her. She sought to walk towards the bedroom door, but Daytona grabbed her by the arm and snatched her back.

"Daytona, let go of me!"

"You really walkin' off while I'm talkin' to your dumb ass!"

"Ariyah's been crying all night! I need to go see about her!"

"Damn that baby!"

"She's your daughter too!"

"That's to be debated!"

Astrid clenched her fists. She knew exactly where this quarrel was headed. Daytona, no matter the size of the facade that he put on in front of his men, was a man dealing with insecurities bigger than his frame.

Standing just over six feet tall, Marvin "Daytona" was a beige shaded man with an extremely muscular frame and reddish, copper hair. The shade of his eyes was the shade of a harsh sunset. His tone was almost lion-ish, and his attitude was of high arrogance. He was the most sexually, alluring man Astrid ever possessed, and she hated him for it. His persona, the way he was, is what drew her in two years ago. Astrid wished like hell she would've kept walking instead of answering the cat call.

I should've kept walking that day, Astrid thought like always in the moment before the storm. *I should've kept walking that day and never looked back. What the hell was I thinking?*

"If I'm so bad for you then why be with me?" Daytona smirked menacingly. "I believe the question is the other way around. We both know who's keepin' who. But I see you need me to remind you of that!"

Traditionally, it was Daytona who threw the first punch, striking Astrid off balance. But just as quickly as she was knocked down, she summoned up enough strength to bounce back and retaliate.

With everything she had, Astrid fought back at the man who was more than a giant to her plus size frame. She fought at him and every other man who ever hurt her that she couldn't see until eventually succumbing to a strength far greater than hers. Time seemed to escape ever so slowly during those moments of Daytona's fists pounding into her flesh.

"Do yourself a favor. Don't go bleedin' all over my damn kitchen floor while you cookin' my dinner," Daytona spat before exiting out of the bedroom. He continued to wipe the blood on his knuckles along the fabric of his pants as he did so.

Astrid lay in a fetal position bleeding into the carpet beneath her. She laid there long enough to suck up her own tears. Long enough to overhear Daytona cooed playfully back and forth with baby Ariyah. And like the innocent, adorable infant she was, Ariyah cooed back at her father as if she was never crying up a storm of her own.

Between the stomach tumor, and the man she loved, Astrid wasn't sure which one would kill her first.

"I swear, I'm so over this damn tax collection gig," Jenny remarked from the bathroom stall. "I got panties that's worth more than what I make here in a year."

"Sounds to me like you just need to buy a new set of panties." Marissa replied from the next stall over.

"No. It sounds like I need to find a richer husband..."

The two co-workers laughed loud enough for their voices to bounce off the walls of the lady's restroom. They were full of their traditional morning humor, and as usual, Astrid didn't get the memo.

Standing in front of the mirror, she stared into her reflection before her. Had been for the last fifteen minutes of the time she arrived. She was struggling to find some type of life in herself but just as quickly as she tried, she realized that goal was dead before it even started. It was moments like these when she found herself longing for the gentle touch of her sweet Ariyah. She could see her hazel browns in the pools of her own honey brown eyes.

Just an hour ago, before dropping her off at Little Angels Daycare, Astrid hugged her baby extra-long. She pressed her lips along her delicate cheek and inhaled her baby scent. Baby Ariyah giggled and gently chewed on Astrid's chin in loving retaliation. She didn't put up a fuse the way she usually did as she was handed over to one of the workers.

You know mama needs a break this morning, Astrid thought at that moment. *I'm going to do my best to keep hanging on for you.*

She rubbed self-consciously at the swollenness of her full lips. No amount of makeup could hide the impending flaw, but it did manage to do small wonders for the dark rings that formed underneath her eyes from the night before. There wasn't much for her to hide in plain sight. Daytona wasn't only a man who didn't spare his hits, but he was also smart enough not to plant bruises for everyone to see.

At thirty years of age, Astrid was the epitome of ebony beauty just as her deceased sister, Blu, had been. Standing at five feet and five inches tall, and two-hundred and fifty-five, she bore skin the color of caramel with eyes as brown as fresh honey. A bridgeless nose framed her face with delicate precision, and her full lips bore the shape of a well-defined heart. Locs, the same honey shade as her eyes, sprouted gracefully from her roots and made a well-groomed branchy river midway down her back. She was a black Queen. But the current state of her mind and years of unforgiveness blinded Astrid from seeing everything she could possibly see in herself.

"Screw a rich husband," Marissa dismissed as she exited out of the stall. "Just get you an old hustler, have his baby and then watch his ass die."

Jenny cackled over the flushing of the toilet before exiting out of her stall as well.

Astrid didn't look in either one of her co-worker's directions. Instead, she busied herself with finding her ChapStick inside of her purse. Her distance was anything but new. Most of her co-workers took it as Astrid not being an early bird. But as always, there were some who felt the need to bring their perkiness to her world and Jenny and Marissa were the types.

"Long night, beauty queen?" Jenny inquired as she came over to the sink to wash her hands.

"Something like that," Astrid replied dryly as she sought ruthlessly for her ChapStick at the bottom of her purse.

"I could definitely stand to say the same," Marissa chimed in. "My husband came in last night from his week-long business trip ready to set me ablaze and y'all know the ending to that..."

Pausing in her quest, Astrid looked up at the nagging woman with high annoyance. "No, Marissa. I don't."

Marissa cocked an eyebrow. "Sex, Astrid."

"Is there a reason why you feel like I need to know that?"

"I swear, it wouldn't be a good morning if you didn't reply so bitterly and dry to my sex stories, dear, Astrid." Marissa blew off. "Obviously, one of us didn't get her feather ruffled the right way last night."

Astrid ignored her and went back to fetching for her ChapStick again.

"Hey...you alright?" Jenny asked, placing a hand on her back. "It's donuts in the breakroom if you need a happy tune up."

"Fine," Astrid replied plainly. "And no thank you."

Finally retrieving her ChapStick, Astrid went about gently

coating her lips. "Aww, honey. Is your lip swollen again?" Jenny frowned.

"Allergies..." Astrid replied quick-witted. It was her usual alibi. One that was always very much believable to the likes of Jenny because she often suffered from allergies during the summertime.

Marissa on the other hand was wiser than that. "If you say so..." she remarked, plucking at the curls in her blonde hair.

Pausing in her lip coating, Astrid looked over at her. "Is there something you would like to say to me, Marissa?"

Peering over at her in the mirror, Marissa didn't respond. Instead, she rolled her eyes and exited out. She would save her commentary for the other co-workers to marvel at and gossip about.

"Don't mind her ass, Astrid," Jenny interjected. "Did you go buy that ointment I told you about?"

Astrid pulled her eyes away and back to her task at hand. "I ran out. Gotta get more."

Jenny stared back at her thoughtfully. Astrid dared to look back at her too just as she had done Marissa. "Boyfriend wasn't aware that I was allergic to the ingredients in the lipstick he bought me. I didn't think anything of it myself. So...now. Here we are."

Eventually, a careless smile spread across Jenny's face and Astrid immediately found herself relieved. She wasn't into getting the third degree from women she only knew about on the clock. Snapping made her look guilty and being silent made her out to be a weak link. She didn't care for either emotion no matter how she felt.

"Anyway, I guess I should warn you before we get to our stations. Mrs. Baxter is on one today." "Again."

"Yes. Possible firing spree. She got rid of two yesterday. You've already called out once this week to go with the last. Just giving you a heads up. Keep your eyes plastered to the computer."

Astrid waited until Jenny was out of the bathroom to look at her reflection once more. Beneath the foundation, she could see the mild discoloration of her skin. The pain that crippled her last night was nowhere to be found, yet she could feel herself hanging on by a thread. She could see life slipping from her eyes. The mystery always seemed to brew to the surface; how did she become this woman before her? What she knew was that long ago someone stole something valuable from her and she had yet to find her way back.

Dropping the ChapStick back into her purse again, Astrid retrieved her medicine. Last night, after their violent quarrel, Daytona hid her pills. He was often evil that way. And Astrid would wake up in the middle of the night hunting for it. This time, they were hidden underneath the kitchen sink.

Popping the top, Astrid took two pills and chased it down with water from the sink. Closing her eyes, she inhaled in an attempt to ready herself for a day she wasn't ready for. At the same time her cell phone buzzed, alerting her of a message. She reached into her rose, pink skirt pocket and looked at it. The number displayed was unknown, but she knew the sender very well.

Grand rising, Astrid Montgomery. I won't bother asking if this is a good time to reach out to you. My Deja Vu always reminds me just how lethal your words are. Then again, so are mine. I probably shouldn't bury the stress of this confession on you, but I've been on a clairvoyant ass train lately. You've been in my dreams. I'm guessing the safest thing for me to say—or better yet, ask, is if you would consider reaching out to me? At least let me know how you're living?

— Z.K.

Empty Birthdays
ZANE

"So this is your answer? You gon leave me to handle life on my own?"

Zane's eyes burned from the tears he was holding back in the effort of getting his words out. Man was it hard. He needed to stay strong in the midst of the event unfolding before him. Growing up in the streets of Saxton, he encountered some excruciating things. Not giving a damn who claimed to be the toughest of the tough when it involved him and the powerful men, he kept the blocks warm for. Still, none of the amount of years of running wild, and belligerent, prepared him for what was taking place before him.

Beneath the dark midnight sky of his beloved Saxton city, on the Western Bridge, Zane and his twin brother, Gabe, seemed to have been breathing fire back and forth at each other like dragons for the last half hour. For the first time in all of the years they spent bonding, fighting and bonding again, Zane found himself at a permanent pit stop. He was tired in a way that left him straining, fighting against his own tears.

"You don't get it, Z!" Gabe cried as he inched further back on the edge of the bridge's ledge. In his left hand, he held a gray revolver which he intended to use on himself. His eyes were glassy, and full of dark things Zane couldn't unlock the way he usually did. "I been on my fucking own since we were born!"

"No, you haven't! Nigga I been here!" Zane barked. His hands were balled so tight he could feel them going numb. He could feel himself falling apart.

"I'm the one who had to deal with the treatments! The medication! Not you! And now I gotta deal with this shit eatin' at me!"

"Gabe, will you just tell me what the hell are you talking about?"

"I can't burden you with that, big brother. Just know, I'm sorry. Keep your eyes on the snakes around you..."

"Gabe!"

Zane watched his brother inch farther to the edge of the bridge's ledge. His heart thumped wildly out of his chest, and he struggled like hell to breathe. It felt as though he was about to drown.

"Gabe, baby brother, I got you! I've always had you! Think about this shit!"

"I can't live with what I did!" Gabe cried. "It's killin' me! I'm sorry, Z!"

"We in this shit, man! We in this shit together! Gabe! No!"

The moment Gabe pressed the gun to his temple and fired off, Zane felt his own breath snatch out of him. Sparks from the gun mixed with blood and brain matter decorated the air. Gabe's eyes fluttered upwards into his head and his body fell backwards down into the water 700 feet beneath the bridge.

Silence wrapped itself around Zane like a harsh wet blanket. He stood frozen until he heard the crucial blow of his brother's body crash into the body of water.

The tears that burned at his eyes flowed down his face just in time for the wind to come sweeping through and blow them along his skin with no sense of direction. At the age of twenty-four, his twin brother was dead. And he had to live with it...

Zane Keys sat calmly, but annoyed, inside of his office at the Keys Resort. The plan was to start his day by sitting in the space in which he occupied until he knew what to do with himself. Mind his business apart from the usual workload. Sip on the morning coffee his secretary, Honey, brewed for him. He wasn't in the mood for anything, or anyone.

The thought of vacating to a place on his private yacht where he couldn't be found like always when the workload became mundane crossed his mind the moment he woke up. He wasn't sure why he didn't listen to it. Then again, he did. Too much alone time on this particular day opened him up to far too many unwanted thoughts. The two Caucasian men sitting before him dressed in suits crisp enough to roll quarters on currently had him questioning his sanity though.

Their names were Volmer and Colton Ryan, also known as the wealthy Ryan brothers in the high circle of savvy businessmen throughout the white parts of Saxton. The weight of their reputation made them cocky.

However, at the moment, the confident brothers were both wearing smug expressions at the noncompliance of Zane. What was supposed to be their next victim in being illiterate in business was backfiring on them horribly.

"Our negotiations are always top tier," Volmer protested in the most professional voice he could find. "We pay out the big bucks, and our consumers get to retire before they can even begin to consider it."

Taking a draw from his cigar, Zane glared at both men. They fit the exact profile of walking upper class wealth with not a care in the world except which color suit they needed to get pressed in an ample amount of time to go swindle a color folk.

Financially, Zane could very much identify but he hadn't been born into it. He didn't always have money at his fingertips, and it was that very reason why he was more than annoyed with the proposal at hand. For the last few weeks, the bougie vets hunted him down and he chose today to entertain them.

Leaning back in his velvet office chair, Zane released a perfect ball of smoke from his lips, and it floated up to the ceiling to rest along with his thoughts. "I purchased the Wilcomb property for far more last year. I'm making back three times as much as that. Frankly, I find both of you fellas' offers to be insulting, but that's hardly why I'm saying no."

"You don't trust that our blueprint for a more convenient medical center will make up for any of your future plans?" Colton inquired.

"No," Zane replied in a raspy baritone.

Sitting across the room in one of the office chairs, Honey cleared her throat, and Zane stole a glance over at her. With a sharp eyebrow, his secretary pursed her lips tightly and tapped her finger on her wrist watch, alerting him of the time. The signal meant he had a far more important visitor or a phone call to tend to. More than likely, both.

"Mr. Keys..." Volmer spoke.

Zane looked back to the men before him, prompting them to continue on with their salesman tactic. "Wouldn't you like to be able to have another tag under your belt? Imagine if the city of Saxton not only knew how much of a saucy businessman you are when it comes to building from the ground up, but also that you are an asset in helping to invest in the medical well-being of its locals."

"That's a pretty ass picture you just painted," Zane mused dryly. "But trust me, my city is well aware."

Colton smirked. "How far into the community can you trace that claim?"

"Not as far back as you two brothers obviously. But I can guarantee you my path isn't traced back to the involvement of ownership of cotton fields."

Both brothers coughed hard enough for their faces to shift slightly red.

"Mr. Keys," Colton interjected nervously. "We don't operate from that spectrum."

"It doesn't matter. That's the spectrum you're from."

"Can you at least tell us the real reason for your lack of interest?"

"I don't trust your business moves. Mrs. Abram, a past customer of yours—I'm sure you two have not forgotten because you're both so genius. You both promised her that her father would be safe where he was at the Glorious Hills Retirement home before you decided to make it over. Did you not?"

"Mr. Keys, we had to remodel. That was the deal."

"The deal was to turn the home over into better living quarters. More spacious, more vibrant. You gentlemen, or whatever the fuck you call yourselves, took it upon yourself to not only build the rooms smaller but set in place financial qualifications and bogus ass rules that you knew wouldn't guarantee some of the same tenants who were there before. Black tenants."

"You're making this a race issue?"

"I'm making it a race issue because that's what it is, Mr. Ryan. You both lied about the blueprints you showed to Mrs. Abram. And in return she lost out big. But it's all gravy. I repaid her and her father back big."

The tan skinned men both stared back at Zane with grudged expressions. "You made some middle-aged woman's issue, your issue," Colton remarked.

"She's a middle-aged black woman. A widow. With five grand-kids. She is my issue."

"If you plan on getting more money, Mr. Keys, you're going to have to step on some toes."

"Well, then. Let me make you two the first. Both of you, get the fuck out of my office."

The Ryan brothers, stone faced and red, uncomfortably cleared their throats before collecting their briefcases and standing to their feet.

"This won't be the last time we meet, Mr. Keys." Volmer told him. "For your sake, the both of you should hope that it is."

"It was nice attempting to do business with you," Colton added. He held out his hand to Zane, but his supposed formal act of departure wasn't received back.

Gathering their pride, the men exited out of the office leaving their confidence behind.

At thirty years of age, not only was Zane intimidating in business, but his overall appearance was also enough to frighten or entice depending on the company he kept.

He stood at 6'4", two hundred forty pounds with mocha brown skin. His eyes were a delicate set of hazel browns. A beard shielded his face, and he sported a low-cut fade. Two significant tattoos were imprinted on his skin; his only daughter's name, Sage, graced his left arm and Gabe reserved a space on his upper left chest. Zane was a beautiful, full figured black man, who's body art was reserved only for off hours alongside his other acts. Well, the ones he felt like doing lately.

"I have never seen such a bold pair of vultures," Honey remarked as she stood from her chair.

"You'd think it's 1954, the way they came strolling in here."

"They're the usual market faces," Zane brushed off. "Plenty of them. You know they're right. They're going to come back. They always do."

It wasn't the first time Zane was approached with a bogus offer. Being a businessman meant you were prone to being a target for sharks. His father, Morris Keys, taught him better than that.

Not only did Zane have a successful five-star hotel, his gentleman's club, the Red Lace, resided in the heart of Saxton. There was also the Cigar Palace in which he ran in partnership with Blaze Rushmoore of BloodRush Casino. The previous owner was more than willing to let the two men buyout and flip. Zane promised them fifteen percent, and he delivered. His financial reputation was through the roof based on his business relationships alone.

But while Zane was successful in all those things, and then some, there was a hole in his heart centered around two people. One of them was his late twin brother, Gabe. The Ryan brothers picked a fine day to screw with him. It was his thirtieth birthday and would've been Gabe's as well. The weight of his death still weighed on Zane like boulders after six years.

"Mia called while you were in the middle of your business meeting," Honey said.

Zane licked his lips thoughtfully. "How'd she sound?"

"Stressed out. Whatever that daughter of yours did this time had her balling."

Putting out his cigar in the ashtray, Zane digested the words and rubbed thoughtfully at his beard. "That's not all," Honey walked closer to him. "Ring called. You know he and Blaze got something set up for you tonight at your club? Donovan's idea of course."

"I'm aware."

"This mean you're actually going to celebrate your birthday this year?"

"No. It doesn't."

"You only turn thirty once."

"You plan on digging up my brother to join me?"

The question was rhetorical. But the expression on Honey's face told that she was offended.

"My apologies, Honey." Zane apologized. "This just isn't a good day for me."

"I understand. Should I call your men up and tell them to can everything?"

"No."

Planting her hands on her hips, Honey nodded. "Also, Mrs.

Rushmoore called. She's downstairs sitting in Belvedere. Said she'd wait as long as she needed to until you were done."

Eventually, Zane nodded. "Do me a favor, Honey. Hold any other calls and requests today. Mrs. Rushmoore is the only other person I plan on seeing."

Honey nodded firmly. "Another cup of coffee? I can add some Hennessy to it this time?"

The idea was tempting, but Zane shook his head tentatively. "No."

As soon as Honey excused herself out, Ring called up Mia. She answered on the first ring. It was also obvious that she was a wreck and intoxicated.

"Zane," Mia spoke. Her tone was fragile. Giving away that she was still in the middle of crying.

"Mia, what happened?"

"What isn't happening? There's something wrong with our daughter. I don't know what but she's...she's...."

"Mia. Breathe."

A brief silence fell over the line, but eventually, Mia began speaking again. "She's just so moody all the time. She broke the kitchen window. I'm at my wits end, Zane."

Zane's eyes scattered over to the hand drawn picture of a ballerina hanging up on his office wall. He tugged thoughtfully at his beard. "Where is she?"

"At a friend's house."

"A friend's house..."

"Yeah," Mia replied lazily. "Some girl named Carla. Stays over in Balorn Communities. I'm letting her sleep over there for the next two days. I'm losing her, Zane. She isn't even fifteen yet and I'm already losing her."

"You're not losing her, Mia."

"Then what do you suggest?"

"Give her some space."

"You're asking me to give our twelve-year-old daughter space? In a city like this? Did you not hear a single fucking word I just said? She broke my damn kitchen window. It took everything in me not to beat her ass where she stood."

Zane remained quiet as Mia recalled the events of what happened between her and Sage. Apparently, their daughter arrived home from school off the city bus and walked into the house without saying a word to her mother. The lack of acknowledgement resulted in Mia verbalizing her feelings of offense and having to clean up broken glass in return because Sage had gotten so upset at her she shoved her fist through it.

"How bad was she hurt?"

Mia sighed. "Not bad," she mumbled. "Four stitches and a wrap."

"Mhmm. Mia, if you push, she'll only push back."

"That's some old school bull shit talk that's never worked."

"It's either that or you let her come stay with me. And we've both been down that road. You don't wanna loosen your grip."

"I don't want my baby around those grown ass women you like to play house with. That's not the example I'm aiming for here."

"And you think her seeing her own mother drink herself into oblivion is a good look?"

"I'm not drinking."

"Mia, don't bullshit me. And for the record, I wouldn't just bring a random woman around Sage."

"I know you."

"No. You don't."

For the first few years of Sage's life, Zane wasn't present, and it wasn't by choice. He only came to know of his daughter's existence several years ago. Mia showed up at his doorstep with a quiet, yet observant little Moroccan brown skinned girl in tow and Zane caught on. His ways were bound to catch up to him sooner or later. It was the candid features of his mother that gave Sage away.

Zane stepped into the role of fatherhood immediately, but it was the lack of his presence that often made Mia forget the type of man she was dealing with. The Zane Bryan Keys who resided on Kissmett street had grown into another breed of a man. He was no longer Z the street hustler who changed females like he changed his boxers. He still had his selection of women, no doubt. A man as mouthwatering as him, it would be a sin for him not to. But his nymphomaniac, bad boy ways were long gone.

"That's not what I meant, Zane." Mia went on to claim.

"It's in your tone what you meant. But I didn't call to argue. You're worried about our daughter." "And you aren't?"

Zane fell quiet. Worrying wasn't the emotion he was feeling. He was troubled. Had been for a while. For the last two months, his twin brother was constantly popping up in his dreams, and strangely, Sage would be there as well. The nightmares began around the time Mia first came to him about their daughter's erratic behavior. Bipolar wasn't historic in the Keys family. To his knowledge, Gabe was the only one diagnosed with it.

"Zane..." Mia spoke again. "What if...?" she attempted to ask. It was obvious what she was alluding to. What if their daughter was suffering from some form of Bipolar disorder just as his brother Gabe had? Mia's emotions beat her there. The phone line became riddled with muffled cries, and Zane did his best not to give into his own emotions.

"Listen, Mia. Whatever it is, we'll deal with it. I'll make an appointment when we get off."

∽

The luxurious Keys Resort, a temporary homing ground for both locals and tourists alike, sat at the waterfront of the Belmont Sea giving a broad view of its harbor. To get there by car, visitors traveled a road leading fifteen minutes out of the Saxton city limits. But for the surrounding communities, such as the nearby beach houses, by foot, there was a pedestrian bridge and then a short nature trail through woods and ultimately a boardwalk.

Within the Keys Resort, the tall building exuded gold and beige walls, red velvet carpet and crystal marble flooring. It consisted of sixteen floors. Gold lion statues and white painted, circular cement pools gave a view of elegant ancient interior. There was a massive food court, breakfast bar and a social area for stayers with an appetite for finger food and alcohol.

Entertainment amenities consisted of two large tennis courts, three family pools, a three-hundred-acre golfing field and a banquet room. The Belvedere Restaurant, often the main entertainment area during the night hours, resided on the bottom floor with an overview balcony of the surrounding area. It was the exact location Zane starred in as he exited out of the hotel lobby through the double automatic doors.

The misty air kissed his mocha skin as he searched along the view of people immersed in conversation over brunch. In the far right, a dark-skinned full-figured woman sporting shades, a pink neck scarf and a wide brim sun hat sat at a table. She took a sip of her cold beverage before looking up in Zane's direction and waving her hand in the air, signaling him over.

Adjusting the collar on his gold silk shirt, Zane swiftly made his way over to her through the maze of tables.

"Serenity." He greeted her.

"Zane," she greeted back delicately. "I was hoping this wasn't a bad time."

"For you. Never."

Serenity Rushmore stood at her feet to wrap her arms around him. Pushing up on the tips of her toes, she brushed her lips softly along his cheek. "Happy birthday," She whispered. "I don't assume that this day is easy for you."

Zane squeezed her back warmly. "It's a day."

Serenity cupped her hand along his face and took in the pinch of sadness in his eyes. "You should not be working on your birthday. But I know that's easy for me to say."

"It's all good."

"Is it really?"

Zane gently squeezed her hand in reassurance. "Come on. Sit down."

Nodding, Serenity reclaimed her seat. Zane followed by sitting in the chair across from her.

"Just so you know, I warned my husband not to buy into your man Donovan's birthday antics. Along with Ring, they all seem to have this obsession about you being swept away by some lady of the evening as if it'll make everything better."

"Spoken like a woman." Zane mused.

Zane and Serenity's friendship hadn't been difficult to come by. In fact, it often felt like fate to Zane. Their frequent meetups began through his connection with Blaze, Serenity's husband. Through their business partnership, the two men formed a brotherhood. Aside from he and Donovan's frequent visits to the BloodRush Casino, the men also frequented the Cigar Palace every other night where they shared conversation over cigars and beer.

It was during one of those particular hangouts that Serenity was present, and Zane fell into the temptation of inquiring about the possibilities of her being in association with Astrid due to the past events surrounding the murder of her late sister. Zane often asked about Astrid through conversations here and there with her older sister, Sky, but he could never bring himself to dig too far.

Serenity, however, was an open book. She hadn't admitted it right away out of respect. But eventually, a phone call was made to Zane.

"I'm just calling it how I see it," Serenity went on to say. "But I'll steer away from that war." The two exchanged laughs for a short moment, and then reclaimed their poise.

"I spoke to Astrid last night," Serenity revealed. "Did you make up your mind on reaching out to her?"

"Yes."

"How'd that go?"

"She hasn't responded. I don't expect that she will." A serious expression masked Serenity's face.

"What is it?" Zane asked.

"I think...I know. She's in trouble."

"Based on what you've shared with me over the course of time, Serenity. I figured that. Men like Daytona never come without repercussions."

Serenity shook her head. "No. This is different."

Zane leaned in. "How so?"

"She's...sick. I refrained from sharing that part of her life. But Astrid is ill." "How bad?"

"Stomach tumor. She has her down moments when we talk. But last night, she sounded so hollow. I've been trying to talk her into coming back to Saxton."

Zane grunted. "Good luck with that."

"I think my luck is much larger than you think."

Zane tore his attention away from Serenity and planted his eyes out on the view of the harbor. It'd been twelve years since he last saw Astrid. A majority of their adolescent years were spent being each other's worst enemy. At least that's how Astrid saw him. Zane never felt that when it came to her. "Reaching out to her this morning, it honestly hasn't been my first time. Ever since you gave me her information six months back, I've been sending messages."

"She wants help, Zane. She just doesn't know how to get it. She's afraid. Which is where you come in. I need a favor."

Zane looked back to Serenity. "And that is?"

"Come with me to Daytona."

"I'm not sure if that's the best thing."

"You sound like Blaze."

37

"Blaze is right."

"I hear you, Zane." Serenity told him. She reached underneath her scarf and tugged at her white crystal necklace. "I hear you both. But I'm telling you, I can feel it. Something isn't right. This won't end right for Astrid. I refuse to let her go out like her sister. I owe her that much."

"Even if you're right. What is my presence going to do?"

"Seeing you may persuade her."

Zane scoffed. "My face is the last thing Astrid would want to see."

Zane recalled the stressful three months Astrid was inside of Stanton Memorial Hospital after the rape. The visits.

The time he often spent praying to God she didn't get lost on the other side. For the longest, he tried to make himself forget the hell she went through.

Falling into a coma.

Missing her graduation.

Losing her scholarship to Harvard University.

When Astrid did finally awaken, the light that once resided in her eyes was stolen. Zane never forgot the feeling of his own heart breaking at the realization; nothing about her was the same.

"Can you at least think about it?" Serenity requested gently. She reached over and grabbed his hand. "Who's to say it wouldn't help you."

Zane digested Serenity's words. "I'll think about it." He told her.

Waves

ASTRID

"Gilbert Tax Services Department. This is Customer Service Rep, Astrid Montgomery speaking."

"It's nice of you to finally call your big sister and tell her happy belated anniversary," Trina spoke.

Astrid rattled her fingers lightly along the computer's keyboard out of annoyance. "Hello, Trina."

"Surely I can get a better greeting than that. Been all of two months since I've heard from you. That's a sad ass pattern, but I'll pick another day to complain about that."

"How about you not?"

"I still haven't gotten my happy anniversary."

Leaning back in her chair, Astrid sighed. "Happy anniversary, Trina. Care to remind me of the first time you and Lance actually had sex?"

"You wish. And thank you little sister. I'm now convinced that you love me just a little bit more by at least five percent."

"Happy to be of service. Now what do you want?"

Trina chuckled dryly into the phone. "Damn, Astrid. Can I get at least five minutes with you?"

"I'm at work."

"Obviously. I would call you when you get off, but you don't answer. I shouldn't have to receive updates on my own sister through her thuggish ass beau."

Astrid parted her lips to speak but paused when she saw her boss walking down her row. Her coworker, Jenny, wasn't lying. For the last three days now, Mrs. Baxter was on a firing binge only to have new faces already in place to occupy the empty spaces. The irritating woman watched Astrid as though she were contemplating her being on the list for the pink slip. Because of that, Astrid held her tongue and pretended to be busy with inputting information on the screen before her until her boss was officially out of earshot.

"Hello?" Trina tugged from the other end.

"Yep," Astrid replied glumly. "I'm here."

"How are you?" she asked softly.

Astrid hated it when her sister asked her that question. As a matter of fact, she despised the question in general. Just what the hell did it really mean? If one was to be honest, would the person asking be ready for the revelation?

How am I doing? I'm fucking dying. My daughter is going to be left without a mother. I'm getting my ass beat every other day by a man who swears he loves me and I'm on a thin line to unemployment...

Closing her eyes, Astrid forced herself to quiet her thoughts, and settled on the cliche' response. "Fine."

"You always say that."

"Okay. I'm good." Astrid reworded with dry humor.

"You always say that too."

Astrid rubbed tiredly at her temples. "Trina, can I please call you back?"

"No, because I know you won't. And plus, this phone call is important."

"Please. Oblige me."

"I'm having an anniversary party next weekend for grandma and grandpa. Isn't it neat that me and Lance's were so close to theirs? I'm praying we end up fifty years deep."

"Yeah, that's nice. I won't be able to make it."

"Bitch, you didn't even wait for me to tell you the full information."

"It doesn't matter, Trina. I've missed a few days at work. Which means I'll be spending my weekends making it up. It explains why I'm here right now."

"You can't pick one weekend to come celebrate with your family, Astrid?" Trina asked in a wounded tone. "The very two people who've been our safety net."

Astrid hated it when her sister did that too. One minute she could be as harsh as winter and the next, her tone could go softer than snow white.

"I will try. Okay?" Astrid told her. She was very aware of what their grandparents were to them all of their lives. Losing their parents at a young age to a drunk driver had not been easy on any of them. It was their beloved sister Blu who took it the hardest. She'd gotten so caught up in the wrong parts of life that it backfired.

"I miss you, Astrid," Trina spoke after a moment. "I mean that shit. It's been a while since you've been here and I'm describing that length of time with very little emphasis."

"Trina..."

"No one is going to get you here. You know I'd kill for you. Me and Sky, both."

"Okay, no! We will not talk about that right now!" Astrid replied abrasively.

"If not now then when, Astrid? It's been years."

"Years in which you don't get to throw in my face!"

Astrid wasn't aware how pitchy her voice had gotten until one of her nearby co-workers, Linda, across from her in her cubicle, cleared her throat. It was hard enough to catch Astrid's attention. Looking back at her, Astrid followed Linda's finger as she pointed over in their boss's direction where she was now surrounded by three white women. They were all dressed in suits, and sported expressions stern enough to cut ice.

Upper management, she noted.

Sighing, Astrid turned back around to face her computer screen. "Trina, I really have to go."

"I just need one more minute."

"What?"

"Zane asked about you."

"Oh..." Astrid mumbled. A small ball of heat settled in the bottom of her stomach.

"Yeah. He wanted to know the usual. How life is treating you down in Daytona. He made the local newspaper again this week. That man is making a hell of a living, I swear."

"That reminds me that I should curse you out for giving him my number."

"Astrid, I've told you a thousand times. I have no idea how the man got your number. But maybe it's a sign that you should hit him up sometime. You do owe him that you know."

"Maybe, Trina. Okay. Anyway, I have to go. I'll call you later."

"Promise?"

Astrid rolled her eyes. "Yes. I promise. And don't be sending Sky to blow up my phone either. That'll only piss me off."

"Fine, Astrid."

After hanging up the phone, Astrid tried her best to busy herself by catching up on her spreadsheets as she'd done before the phone call from her bothersome sister. For a while, it worked. But it wasn't enough to keep her mind off of Zane. Now she had another reason to be annoyed other than being at work on a Saturday morning.

Astrid was never over the moon when it came to hearing from either one of her big sisters. But unlike Trina, Sky rightfully kept her distance. She communicated through mail every holiday like a faithful distant sibling. Trina on the other hand wasn't that type. She needed contact. She was always that way.

The truth was, Astrid hated talking to her sister because she knew where the conversation would lead. Trina would guilt-talk her into coming to Saxton knowing her request would be denied. Somewhere along the way, Zane would come up. She never expected news about Donavan. The two of them, per her request, ended their friendship just months after the incident.

Astrid chewed skittishly at her lower lip. The tips of her fingers itched as she pounded the keys before she finally gave in to the plaguing curiosity mounting her.

Clicking out of the spreadsheet and onto the main internet browser, Astrid typed in Saxton City, followed by Keys Resort. Her heart palpitated at the image of Saxton City's quoted most eligible, single and hardworking man, Zane Bryan Keys. He stood, cockily. Back strong and chin up in front of a large sign that read Keys Resort, Luxury Hotel & Beach Houses. The headline above the picture read Luxury Hotel Continues to Attract Out of State Tourists; More Business For Belmont Sea Local Fisher & Boatmen.

In a well pressed gray suit flawlessly supporting his husky frame, Zane smiled boldly in a way that got underneath Astrid's skin. She could smell the arrogance. He was always a street alpha male of many choices, and an attitude to match it.

Reaching into her lower drawer, she retrieved her cellphone and pulled up the message he'd sent her a few days ago. Above were other previous messages she'd yet to reply to from several months back. Below the message she received from the previous days was a recent one from earlier this morning.

It's me and Gabe's thirtieth birthday, and I feel like I'm going to break, were his only words.

The mystery plagued Astrid. Why did Zane care about how she was? Why was she suddenly his confidant from a distance?

Sucking in air, she returned her cell back to the drawer and clicked out of the image.

When her desk line began ringing, she found herself relieved at the expectation of a possible frustrated customer. Frustrated customers meant she wouldn't be burdened with her own thoughts.

"Gilbert Tax Services Department. Customer Service Rep Astrid Montgomery speaking."

"Good afternoon, Astrid," Serenity greeted warmly.

Astrid adjusted her tone from dead to mildly upbeat. "Serenity...hi."

"I don't mean to disrupt you. I've been calling you on your cell, but it goes straight to voicemail, and I didn't want to run the risk of calling your apartment line. Is everything okay?"

"Umm..."

"Mrs. Montgomery, may I speak with you?"

Looking up from her cubicle, Astrid met eyes with Mrs. Baxter. The look on her face was stern. Her eyes direct. But beneath all of that, there was a mirror of strange distress.

Damn. Here we go. Way to go, Astrid.

"Um, Serenity, I'm going to have to call you back."

"Okay, love. I'll be here at the casino for most of the day today. You do have the number here, yes?"

"Yes, yes, of course."

"Mrs. Montgomery! Now, please!" Mrs. Baxter prompted her more firmly.

Hurrying off the phone, Astrid shot up from her chair quick enough to make her own head spin. She refused to make eye contact with anybody on her way to the boss's office. All the while, she silently prayed this wasn't a pink slip call. She was in no mood to fight with Daytona again. He was surprisingly peaceful enough this morning to not pick a fight with her before heading out of the door to take Ariyah to daycare. Astrid didn't question her boyfriend's calmness. She chose to appreciate it while it lasted. She knew, sooner or later, she would have to deal with the heat.

Entering Mrs. Baxter's office, Astrid halted at the sight of the two policemen who were also present. She frowned, perplexed at their presence. She didn't remember seeing them walk through.

"Have a seat, Ms. Montgomery." Mrs. Baxter told her. Her tone came off fragile as she shut the door and came to sit behind her desk.

Astrid pinned her attention back to her boss. "Huh?"

"Can you please have a seat?" Mrs. Baxter requested of her again.

Damn. I'm getting fired, she thought.

She would definitely need to call Serenity back. Astrid put her on the block list forgetting she also had her work information. It was for her sanity. The temptation of leaving Daytona was too heavy of a weight for her.

Slowly, Astrid sat down in one of the hard chairs. She glanced over at the officers once more.

Both of them, black men, stared back at her with a peculiar sympathy that matched her boss.

"Astrid," Mrs. Baxter spoke, catching her attention again. "Uh, these two policemen here would like to speak with you."

"About?"

One of the policemen stepped forward. "Ms. Montgomery. I'm Officer Bowman. I'm afraid I have some horrible news."

Astrid's eyebrows crinkled in a frown. "News?"

The policemen nodded. "Yes. We do regret coming to your job to deliver this type of information. It's been heavy on all of us."

"What is this about?"

"It's your daughter, Ariyah."

"My baby?" Astrid stood. She could suddenly feel a starting off beat drum inside of her chest. "What's going on? Is everything okay?"

Officer Bowman exchanged glares with his partner before looking back at Astrid. "Uh, unfortunately, there's been a shooting that took place at the daycare she attends."

Astrid stared back silently at the man. She was sure she heard wrong. She laughed sheepishly. "Huh? What are you talking about? Her father dropped her off this morning."

"Yes," The policeman nodded sadly. "The shooting happened an hour ago."

Astrid shook her head. "No. I think you have the wrong Ariyah," she denied.

"It's on the news, Astrid," Mrs. Baxter said. Grabbing the remote off of the desk, she aimed it at the miniature tv that hung up on the wall in the corner.

Looking up at the screen, Astrid took in the scene on the tv screen of the white and cotton blue building that read Little Angel Nursery. Yellow tape blocked it off. White sheets on the ground. Dozens of policemen. Police cars. Parents and strangers both crying hysterically. New reporters. Astrid was recording all of it permanently in her brain to store alongside the other tragic events of her life. Her attention zeroed in on the caption above the brunette-haired woman reporting. It read *twelve injured in a drive-by shooting, at least seven of them, toddlers.*

Looking back at her boss, Astrid took in the distraught glare in the woman's eyes. "I'm so sorry, Astrid..." Mrs. Baxter's voice broke.

Astrid didn't bother to hear anything more from the television, her boss, or the policemen. She winded out of the office with fire on her heels. The two policemen followed out behind her. For the sake of not making a scene they saved their attempts in trying to stop her in her tracks once they got outside. But no matter what distance they went, there was nothing like the piercing scream of a woman who lost her only child, her only baby.

Over the next four months, life was anything but normal for Astrid. Grief enveloped her in its grip, leaving her withering in the waves of insanity.

Across the nation, the story of the Little Angels Daycare Shooting claiming the lives of seven innocent babies and five adults was broadcasted for strangers to mourn; judge. Or flat out brush off as just another senseless murder spree surrounding a drug deal gone bad. Not only were Kilo, Free and Levi all charged with the death of one year old Ariyah, but also the other innocent babies and adults whose lives were stolen. Daytona's men, as well as the other rivals involved, all shared the crucial weight of multiple murder charges. Neither of them would be alive by the time their sentences were up.

The heartbreaking nightmare unfolded repeatedly day by day through television news reports and front-page newspapers. But there was nothing more treacherous than the outcry in the streets of Daytona for the whereabouts of the drug king himself. Marvin "Daytona" had miraculously vanished, and the policemen as well as the citizens of Daytona City searched desperately for him.

As for Astrid, she was hardly aware of her own breathing.

∼

Bang! Bang! Bang!

"Ms. Montgomery!" A hard voice barked from the other side of the door. It was a tone that held authority, but not enough to persuade Astrid to get up.

She lay tucked in her bed underneath a mountain of sour covers, oblivious to the world outside of her. For the last few months, she heard nothing more than her own cries. The sound of her own tears dripping and soaking into the pillow beneath her. Darkness swallowed her up like a lost fisherman inside of a whale. As far as Astrid was concerned, she was a ghost. And so, she remained unmoved by the sound of her landlord, Stefan, who came to harass her about the rent money she owed. She'd paid up the last two months until her funds ran out.

Throughout the course of months, it was her parents, and then her sisters who came to harass her. Astrid ignored them all. The last time she saw any of her family was at Ariyah's funeral. Even then, she remained silent.

"Ms. Montgomery!" Stefan barked again. "I'm going to call the police if you don't open up! Please don't make me go to that extreme!"

Astrid continued to lay still, unmoved by the threat. It wasn't the first time her landlord threatened to call the police on her. She considered that he actually would have merit this time, but there was nothing that could cause her to care.

Eventually, the banging stopped. Astrid was engulfed into a world of silence again. But her desire to be left alone didn't last. After a passing moment, Astrid heard the sound of her front door parting open and footsteps. Snatching the covers from over her head, she listened in at the sound of a set of heavy footsteps treading around. It sounded like more than one person. Looking towards her bedroom door, beneath the under-space of it, she could see the shadow of bodies moving about.

"Astrid!" A familiar voice called out to her. "Astrid, sweetheart! Are you here? It's me!"

The bed beneath her creaked with pressure as she removed herself from it and stood. Walking over to the door, Astrid pressed her ear to it.

"She's obviously not here, baby," a deep voice said.

"Her landlord just said she was."

A ball of anger grew inside of Astrid, and before she could think about it, she snatched her bedroom door open and barged out into the main sitting room where she came face to face with Serenity and her husband, Blaze.

"Astrid..." Serenity spoke, barely audible.

Astrid took in the dark woman standing just a few feet away from her. She was dressed in a full yellow body dress with brown and white fur trimmed boots. The coat she wore fit snugly around her.

Shades covered her eyes. Her hair, a mile long it seemed, was free and streamed down her back to her tailbone like a long silk sheet. A sunflower was pinned to the side of her hair for decoration.

"I got your key from your landlord," Serenity said as she removed her shades.

Astrid continued to stare back at her. Even after all of this time, she'd only seen Serenity and her husband in pictures, but the images hardly did them any justice. Blaze Rushmoore resembled something out of a warrior movie. His features were firm, and his eyes were set hard, yet unintimidating.

"You two shouldn't be here," Astrid told them. She spoke with as much disdain as she could find though her voice didn't come out that way.

"I think we should," Serenity said to her gently.

Astrid parted her lips to speak, but paused when a tear came falling down her cheek. She wiped it away with the back of her hand.

"Astrid," Serenity took a step towards her. "We've all been so worried about you. I'm here to take you home."

Astrid took a step back. "Fuck Saxton."

"You have a right to feel that way. But being here means you're vulnerable to more danger."

"It's been four months. Daytona is long gone."

"We both know that's not true, Astrid."

"Well in that case, you both should go before he decides to bring his trifling ass back."

Serenity smiled softly. "Certainly you don't think me and my husband came unprepared."

Astrid looked over at Blaze, and he nodded at her in reassurance. Parting open the long leather jacket he wore, he revealed the gun locked at his waist. Just as he did, the front door parted open once again and a heavy set of boots stepped in before the person appeared.

Astrid felt the oxygen leap out of her lungs at the sight of Zane. She was suddenly sucked back into a different time zone. Back on the

Swanny ship. Tied to the bed by her captor. Othello was long gone, and the last person she expected was cradling her in his arms. Her thoughts stopped the moment she felt the softness of his lips brush along her cheek. Everything afterwards was a blur.

Closing the door behind him, Zane stared back at her. His eyes, a calm pair of dark browns. "Astrid," he spoke. "What's going on?"

Astrid grunted out of anger before shooting back to her bedroom and slamming the door shut. She couldn't seem to get away fast enough. The moment she did, she burst into a ball of tears. She cried so hard that she didn't hear Serenity enter. Her presence was known to her when she felt Serenity's arms wrap around her. She pressed her face gently to her back.

"Astrid," Serenity said. "Please. Let us help you."

"Everything..." Astrid heaved. "Everything I had...it's gone, Serenity. It's all...gone. My baby is gone. Daytona killed...my baby. There's nothing else for me."

"Ohh, Astrid." Serenity mourned. She pressed her hand along Astrid's back. "There's a lot left for you that you can't see yet. But you have to let go."

Astrid continued to cry until all she had left was heavy breathing. Until her eyes were swollen, and there were no more waves of tears to come. Serenity had yet to let her go.

"I won't leave you here." Serenity told her. "So, either you can come with me, or I stay here. It's your choice."

Astrid sat down on the bed and crossed her arms. "Your husband would never go for that."

Serenity smirked. "You'd be surprised what my husband will do for me."

Shaking her head, Astrid zeroed in on her reflection in the distance of the bathroom mirror. The blinds in the bedroom were closed, but the sun itself was far too stubborn to hide. Its streams of light shined in, giving light to her wretched appearance. She hadn't seen her own reflection in four months. She was sixty pounds lighter than her normal weight. Her locs were matted. Cheeks, sunken in. Dark circles burdened her eyes. Her skin was flushed, and her lips were extremely chapped. There was nothing about herself that Astrid could recognize except the honey shade of her eyes.

"I quit my job the day Ariyah was killed." she revealed. "I'm behind on my rent. I have no money."

"Well, I can't do anything about your job here. Or Ariyah. But the man who was just banging on your door, my husband just paid him off."

Astrid looked back over at her. "What?"

"Yes," Serenity nodded. "Late fees included. You're paid up for the rest of the year."

Tears stung Astrid's eyes once more, and she looked down at her hands. She hadn't planned to hold on to her apartment. She was waiting for Daytona to show up because she planned to kill him and turn herself into the police. She wasn't sure of anything else further in her life because as far as she was concerned, there was nothing else to live for. Getting rid of the man whose spirit seemed to belong to Othello, though, she was very much sure of that.

"You have to pull yourself up," Serenity told her.

Maneuvering her locs away from her face, Astrid grimaced at the pain shooting through her stomach. She closed her eyes. Gripped her hands onto the edge of the bed to breathe. "My shit runs too deep to do that. I'm stuck."

"Astrid," Serenity cupped her chin, tugging her attention up at her. "You never know who God will send to be in the deep with you. And you're not stuck. I refuse to let you. The question is, will you let me help you, sister to sister?"

Astrid was hesitant to answer. It was the look of plea in her eyes that gave her away. "Please?" she whispered.

Serenity smiled before kneeling and wrapping her arms around her.

Hidden Flames
ZANE

"I never should've told that broad where I stay at," Donovan muttered as he lit his third cigar. He took a draw and blew smoke into the air. "If it weren't for the pull I got with Mr. Sam and his wife, he would've given me the ax."

"I would've given your ass the ax regardless." Blaze humored. "Ain't no toxic woman worth losing your way of living over. Let that shit be a lesson."

"Easy for your ass to say. Most women don't know anything but the language of control. Yours is trained."

"My Serenity is as free as they come. Wasn't no trainin' necessary."

"Bullshit," Ring interjected. "Wife or no wife. That broad would've gotten the business on sight."

The four men, Zane, Donovan, Blaze and Ring, all sat at a smoke table inside of the Cigar Palace. They spent the last two hours giving each other the rundown of everything that's taken place in their week.

So far, Donovan had them all beat.

He encountered a real-life fatal attraction that resulted in one of his booty calls showing up at his job down at Ashton Stocks and demanding he return her phone calls. The psychotic move occurred the day after he arrived inside of his bachelor pad and found the woman entangled in his bedsheets.

"I swear," Zane shook his head. "Your ass is going to learn to stop telling these women where you stay on the first night."

"Nah, they need to learn how to take dick and leave." Donovan retorted.

"Or maybe you should learn how to not think with your dick so much." Blaze suggested as a matter of factly.

Donovan shot him an incredulous look. "My nigga, what man you know thinks with anything else?"

"I second that shit." Ring co-signed.

"You came home and found the woman laying in your bed. Naked." Zane pointed out. "And you didn't call the police then?"

"Not until after I fucked her."

"And that, my brotha, is the reason why you almost lost your job." Blaze declared. "She doesn't even have a key."

"Hell nah! Ain't no woman getting a key to my place!"

"So how is it that she got in, Donovan?"

Donovan shot the men an uncomfortable expression before taking a sip of his beer and placing it back down on the table. He wiped off the leftover beer debris before burping. "That's not the point."

"Oh my god!" Zane and Blaze exclaimed in unison.

"So, what you're sayin' is you invited her to be your damn stalker?" Blaze interrogated.

"Hold on, now. In defense of D," Ring vouched with both of his hands raised. "The broad is fine as hell. I met her."

"Exactly," Donovan mumbled. He removed the cigar resting between his lips. "Body stacked like an Amazon. 6'2. Skin flawless like she doesn't bathe in shit but milk and honey."

Zane raised an eyebrow. "Sounds like most women here in Sax

after they've encountered a few thick wallets and a highly qualified doc."

"That's definitely what it sounds like to me." Blaze agreed.

"Y'all gotta remember how long my brother was locked away," Ring said. "Twenty-three fucking years. He had time to master this shit."

Blaze smirked. "Little brother, I'm pretty sure you don't hold much merit in this conversation either considering where you were five years ago."

"Damn," Ring replied solemnly. "You're just going to keep throwing that in my face, huh?"

"Every fucking chance I get." Blaze smiled broadly. "I had MaryLuv for a season. You were stupid enough to marry her."

"Fuck you, alright." Ring shot him the middle finger. "How was I supposed to know I married a psycho?"

"By realizing what type of fabric the woman is. All women ain't to be laid." Zane stated. "That's real, Z." Blaze nodded.

"Nah, nah, hell nah!" Donovan snapped. "Fuck you, Z!"

"Nah, fuck you." Zane laughed. "Sitting here acting like your ass isn't shittin' bricks after you found that woman at your job. Your warning sign came way before the destruction."

"So what? Now your ass has amnesia?"

Zane took a draw from his cigar. "The hell you mean?"

"Blaze and Ring, would y'all like a rundown of the females Z, the ex-hustler, has had."

Zane waved his hand. "That was years ago."

"Years, my ass. There was Sharon, the coochie witch. She's the reason why your ass doesn't like spaghetti to this day. Niecy, the sniffer. You remember her, right? The one who had a thing for stealing, smelling, and storing your underwear in her private diary?"

"Coochie witch? Sniffer?" Blaze repeated incredulously.

"The hell type of dick was you slangin'?" Ring inquired humorously.

"Shall I get started on Mia–

"Hold up," Zane interjected. "I have a daughter with Mia."

"Nigga you ain't with her no more." Donovan mused.

"That still makes her off limits. And besides, all these stories you're recalling and you're missing one thing."

"And that is?"

"I got rid of their asses. You definitely won't find me linked up with those types of women now."

"So, you sayin' you a fucking monk now?"

"Black men aren't monks, D."

"I'm on your side, my boy," Ring concluded. "But uh, I've never seen one myself."

"Shit me either." Blaze added.

Donovan shot them all a glum expression. "So now y'all niggas wanna be literal?"

"You said it," Zane said.

"Y'all know what the fuck I meant?"

"Nah, not really." Blaze shrugged.

"Man, fuck y'all." Donovan blew off. "I got broads and I'm not ashamed of it. Always been that way and I'm not changing up shit for nobody."

"Damn right. You shouldn't." Ring endorsed.

Zane shook his head. "Sounds to me like you may as well go down to the police station and tell them to save your number on speed dial cause your ass is going to have hell of restraining orders on file."

Blaze and Ring both laughed in unison.

The men continued to talk smack to each other for the next half hour. Eventually, Ring excused himself to one of the other sitting areas to socialize with an attractive woman while Blaze took over one of the serving spaces of one of the bartenders as they departed for their breaks.

In the meantime, Donovan took the time to catch Zane up on

his latest illegal heists; the part of his job he refrained from discussing within the confounds of Blaze and Ring.

"Remember Binx from tenth grade before he got expelled from Camden?" Donovan remarked. "Binx from Thirdstory Avenue?"

"Yeah. The hot headed Italian nigga."

Zane inhaled the smoke from his cigar before releasing it to swarm around the overhead light above them. "That's who you've been trading off with? Since when did racist ass Sam start doing business with Italians?"

"Money is money. He ain't that damn pressed to be the head of some Italian kkk. You see he hired me. And shit, according to my boss, that's all I'm doing. Binx has been sliding me extra units."

"For what?"

"Said he likes the way I move. I've been delivering some other products for him."

Zane stared back at the man who always had his back. The only man who was there to guide him through Gabe's death while his parents kept themselves at bay out of their own guilt. When Zane decided he no longer wanted to run the streets and finally take the same road as his father by starting a legit business, Donovan never hassled him with his doubts. Because of this, Zane chose his words wisely out of brotherly love. "I thought you said you were done with that part?"

"Z, I trade jewelry. Illegally." Donovan emphasized. "You really think some drugs will make a difference if I get caught. Which I won't."

"Emmp," Zane grunted. Donovan had a point. But his argument wasn't coming from a place of concern surrounding his partner's extra side dealings apart from his legit living as a stockbroker. He accepted that Donovan was comfortable not living completely honest in such an dishonest world. It was the company he kept.

"Last I checked, aside from our old rival, Langston, Binx always hired his own blood for business."

"Yeah, but this is more personal." Donovan shot him a serious look. Zane leaned in. "For what reason?"

"Mr. Sam got other women. You know that right?"

"Of course. Stingy ass is always harassing my dancers and I end up having to give his ass the boot."

"Yeah, and that stingy ass white bread is getting played by his own wife."

Zane stared at Donovan before connecting the dots. "Binx and Mrs. Sam?"

Donovan smirked in conformation.

"Man, your ass better clear out before you end up in the middle of that crossfire. Binx might be solid, but your boss, that's a crooked one."

"Nah, I ain't worried. But since we talkin' about gettin' caught up in crossfires, your ass better stay clear of Astrid."

Sitting back in his chair, Zane took a draw from his smoke. That was the only thing Donovan ever really judged him on.

"So, it's different for me?" He insinuated.

"I didn't say that."

"Hmmp. You ain't denying it either." Donovan cocked. "She left everybody here in Sax to deal with the aftermath of that shit. Rape. Sounds like she just couldn't handle what I wasn't willing to give her."

"I was there, D. I walked in on her after it happened."

"I'm not saying it didn't happen. I'm saying it wasn't your mountain to climb. And here you are, stepping into the hills again." Donovan carried on. "Twelve years later, and she's still raisin' hell."

"Damn, D. Did you ever consider Astrid a friend?"

"Hell yeah. But somewhere around senior night, I grew the fuck up."

The two men sat without words for a while, allowing the volume of the rap music playing throughout the Palace to fill in the spaces.

"I'm just sayin,'" Donovan said, breaking the silence. "You know what this is reminding me of," he expressed, silently referring to Gabe.

Zane digested his words for a moment. "In defense..." he said. "Serenity asked me to come to Daytona. Astrid's changed, man."

"Still feenin' for her ass like you used to. I'm telling you man, love ain't shit. You may as well screw every fine bitch you see." Donovan pointed. "Just like that one right there over there by the mini pool table in the corner. Table 11."

Zane carried his eyes over in that direction and spotted four women occupying it. One of them, with long lean legs and skin the color of almond, flashed her teeth hungrily at him. She was more than sexy. Seductive. But the problem was, she wasn't Zane's type.

He surveyed over the other women in proximity until his attention landed on the one sitting at the end. She was hardly interested in where she was or who she was with. Her eyes were glued to the cherry stuck at the bottom of her drink.

Looking back over to the almond brown woman, Zane signaled her over.

Smiling even brighter, she stood to her feet and made her way. She twisted hard enough to break a hip. It was catchy enough to catch the attention of every man she passed.

"Hello, Mr. Keys." she spoke, holding out her hand. "I'm Sasha."

"Good evening, Sasha." Zane greeted her. "How are you tonight?"

"Good as hell now that you've called me over here."

Zane smiled mellowly at her. "You look beautiful."

"Why, thank you."

"I was wondering, can you do me a favor?"

"Anything for a big fine ass brotha like you."

"Your friend. Sitting on the end on the left side. What's her name?"

Disappointment stretched across the woman's face. "Huh?" she looked over her shoulder in the woman's direction. "Her?" she pointed.

"Yeah. Her. What's her name?"

"Layla."

Zane nodded. "Tell her to come here."

"What about my other two homegirls?"

"If I wanted them, I would've said that sweetheart."

"Look, we don't just come up to no man we don't know."

"You just did."

The woman shot him another look of disappointment. Instantly, Zane could see through what the real issue was. And it did nothing but make him hungrier. He held his laughter as the woman made her way back over to her table. Her walk was no longer seductive, but that of a woman whose pride was shot.

"You and your damn fetishes." Donovan remarked.

"Trust me, my brother. It's far from a fetish."

The men looked up at the full figured brown skinned woman standing before them dressed in a passion red dress and red high heels to match.

"Layla," Zane stood. He towered breathtakingly over her like most of the women he met. The plush woman smiled timidly up at him. "My friend said you wanted to speak with me?"

"You have any other plans for tonight?"

"What do you want to do?" Layla asked Zane.

Before she stepped out of her bedroom dressed in a pink fur robe. Zane was sitting on her couch inside of her skyscraper drinking wine. Twenty minutes passed since she disappeared into her bedroom, but he didn't rush her. He knew from the bat what type of woman he was dealing with.

Zane stared back at her standing in the corner beside her bedroom door. "What would you like me to do for you?"

Layla smiled shyly. "I don't know. Movie maybe?"

Zane raised an erotic brow. "Dressed like that?"

"Is that really what you want from me? Companionship?"

Layla parted her lips to respond but then thought better of it. "I'm...newly divorced."

Zane nodded. He took another sip of his wine, and then placed the glass down on the table before him and stood. "Take off your clothes," he ordered her.

Layla smiled sheepishly as she dropped her head down. She tugged with caution at the tie on her robe before finally being able to undo it. Removing it, she let it slide down to the floor at her feet before looking back up at Zane.

"All of it..." he told her.

Slowly, Layla removed her pink, lace bra and then slid out of her lace panties. "I've...gained weight."

"You're beautiful as fuck," Zane told her as a matter of factly, taking in her voluptuous frame. He could feel his manhood pressing along the shield of his pants.

"My girls would think I'm crazy for doing this. They were surprised you even looked my way. I admit, I'm not a one night stand type but..."

"You need it."

Momentarily, Layla nodded.

Carefully, Zane walked over to her, closing in the space between them. He gripped his hands along the plushness of her stomach, and gently pressed her back against the door.

"Do yourself a favor, Layla. Get rid of your homegirls."

"Okay..." she replied breathlessly.

For the rest of the night, Zane pleased his lady counterpart. He drove himself into her until her cries filled up every corner of her skyscraper and her neighbors were sure to come knocking her door down due to disturbance. And all the while, the only thing he could wonder was what Astrid sounded like when she was at her peak. He wondered what she tasted like. Felt like. He wondered if he would be good enough to make her forget the violations she's suffered. He wondered about those things over and over until he looked down at the woman who was drowning in ecstasy beneath him and saw her face staring back up at him. He saw every inch of Astrid's features.

The alluring shade of her eyes, and the delicateness of her lips. Before Zane could catch himself, he was lost as well.

∼

The next day, Zane found himself suffering with a hell of a hangover, but he managed to make it through two staff meetings and a few interviews with three aspirins to back him. Sports season was approaching, and he needed to make sure his employees were well prepared for the long and draining hours they would be pulling in.

There was also Sage's doctor's appointment that took place earlier that morning. Surprisingly, his daughter cooperated through her first session of therapy with Dr. Smollett. The change in her was very apparent. She was quieter. More to herself. But anger, he had yet to see.

"Give her a few more sessions with me before jumping to any conclusions," Dr. Smollett told him and Mia both. "She is evidently stressed, but I need more time to determine why."

Zane received the doctor's information well. It was Mia who couldn't seem to shake loose the possibilities of everything surrounding Sage. To give her a break, Zane suggested that their daughter come to work with him.

And surprisingly, Mia agreed.

"I'll keep in touch," Zane told the brown skinned young man sitting before him. "Give me a week."

"Thank you, sir," he stood smiling broadly. "I'd love to work for you."

"I'll definitely keep that in mind."

Once the young man exited the office, Zane leaned his head back along his leather chair and took a deep breath. He closed his eyes for a second and drifted off before the blaring of his office phone disrupted him. Sighing, he pinched at the bridge of his nose before removing the phone from its cradle. "Yeah, Honey. Sage okay?"

"Yes, she's fine." Honey confirmed. "She's, uh, actually, sitting underneath my desk with her earphones on and her face glued into her drawing pad."

"Sounds about right. What's up?"

"You have one more interview."

"I thought I scheduled for only four today."

"She's more of a walk-in."

"No. Tell them to fill out an application and then come back. My interviews are complete for today.

"Okay," Honey replied. The name Ms. Montgomery fell from her lips before fully disconnecting from the line.

"Montgomery?" Zane repeated urgently. "Shit." Hanging up, he called his secretary's line.

"Yes, sir, Mr. Keys."

"Did you say Montgomery? As in Astrid Montgomery?"

"Yes, I did."

"Send her in."

"Okay. Will do."

"And make sure she is the last one. Anyone else who shows up, schedule them for tomorrow. Preferably afternoon."

"Yes sir."

Hanging up the phone, Zane waited anxiously for Astrid's arrival. It slipped his mind that Serenity gave him a heads up just two days ago about her possibly showing up for a job opportunity. Apparently, the last five interviews she went on didn't go in her favor.

Still, he hadn't been sold that she would show up at his establishment.

Grabbing the pin off of his desk, Zane jabbed anxiously at the pin top until he heard the low knock erupt on his office door.

Standing, he adjusted his shirt collar before walking over and opening the office door.

To say that Astrid hadn't changed physically was an understatement. Zane noticed it when they came face to face back in Daytona. But due to her reaction of seeing him, he'd excused himself back out of her apartment that day.

The events that took place in Astrid's life had transformed her. She was always voluptuous, even back in their Camden High years. But these days, she was a woman of a smaller frame. Still, she hadn't lost her beauty. She was so strikingly beautiful that Zane suddenly felt flushed at the sight of her. The hidden flame he suppressed slowly rose to the surface. He was sure of it. Astrid working under him was going to do him more good than her.

"Astrid," Zane smiled softly. "Glad to see you."

Old Faces, Old Wounds

ASTRID

Astrid wanted to run. She wanted to run far away to a place that didn't require responsibility for anything or anyone. But she couldn't. Three weeks in Saxton had not been enough for her to gain her footing to go out anywhere. It was Serenity.

The moment she arrived, she placed Astrid in her and Blaze's mother-in-law suite right outside of their mini mansion. As big and spacey as it was, it was practically another house. Every morning she woke up with the sun shining in her face. A plate full of food to eat over her medication, or mostly what she could tolerate. Music was played. Bath water was drawn, and her hair was tended to.

For the last three weeks, Serenity took care of Astrid from head to toe as though she were her own child. As if she were trying to breathe life back into her. She wouldn't let up until Astrid found herself getting up out of habit.

It was how she found her way inside of grocery stores again. Roaming the city of various clothing stores. It was how she found herself at the doctor's office face to face with a new care physician who prescribed her with better pain medicine. It was how she found herself going to job interviews she barely had the strength to properly communicate in. It was what led her to stand before Zane dressed in a well pressed neutral button up dress shirt, a black pinstripe skirt and shiny black heels holding two blank pieces of paper that read KEY RESORT JOB APPLICATION.

Astrid stared back at him with no idea of what she should say. She did manage to find some words. "I...didn't know you were done with interviews for the day," she spoke. Her voice still didn't sound normal to her, but nonetheless, it was hers to use with no choice in the matter of how it sounded. She handed over the blank application papers to Zane. "I could've come back. I haven't filled anything out yet."

"That won't be necessary," he told her. Zane reached out and took the papers before moving out of the doorway. "Come in."

Clutching her long strap purse to her side, Astrid walked in. She took in the spacey room full of office things, fancy furniture and a large cherry wood desk. A fish tank full of baby goldfish sat in the far corner, and beside it, was a medium sized bookshelf stocked of books, magazines, and travel ports. Her eyes landed on the large portrait of Zane's parents, Morris, and Priscilla Keys beside a hand painting of the Keys Resort. Underneath them, a hand drawn picture of a ballet dancer was pinned with a thumbtack.

"How are you feeling today?" Zane asked as he closed the door behind her and walked over to his desk to sit.

Tearing her eyes away, Astrid looked over at him.

Why does he have to ask that question? Why does he have to be dressed the way that he's dressed? Like some damn male runway model?

"Fine." Astrid mumbled.

"Great to hear. I'm a bit overworked today, myself. But that's a norm for me on a Saturday."

Astrid nodded slightly before looking back over at the hand drawn picture. It looked as though it was done by someone under-aged but well on their way to becoming a well satisfactory artist.

"You like my choice of office decor?"

Peeling her eyes off of the pictures, Astrid looked back at him again.

"If you're wondering about the picture, it's my daughter's. She draws things that she either sees or dreams about. But she's often critical of herself. When she drew that one, and she actually said she liked it, I told her that I would hang it up."

"It's...an office." Astrid replied.

Zane smirked charismatically. "I'll take that. You may have a seat." He pointed to the two chairs in front of him.

Astrid took it.

"Are you thirsty?" he asked.

"Do you normally ask your interviewees that question?"

"Not necessarily. Guess I'm feeling very hospitable."

"No thank you."

Zane nodded. "So, what brings you here to the Keys Resort?"

Astrid sighed and brushed her locs away from her shoulders. "You already know."

"You want me to treat you like my traditional interviews, Ms. Montgomery."

Astrid stared back at him for a moment before adjusting herself more comfortably in the chair. "Shall I start again?" Zane suggested as he stood to his feet. He held out his hand. "Nice of you to have the Keys Resort in mind as your next place of employment. We have great benefits and a very well put together health insurance package."

A slightly amused expression tugged at Astrid's lips, but she tucked it away in the deepest part of herself before it could even begin to fully rear itself.

"You gotta admit. That was good as hell." Zane charmed.

Astrid looked away from him, and down at her hands. Coming here was a bad idea. A very bad idea.

"You want to be so formal like we've never met each other a day in our lives, Astrid," Zane said more seriously.

Eventually, Astrid looked back up at him. She could see the glare of insult in his eyes. Breathing in sharply, and then out, she sat up more properly in her chair. "What brings me here is that I need a job. And I would greatly appreciate it if you could help me. Please."

Zane rubbed thoughtfully at his beard as he reclaimed his chair. "I would love to help you, Astrid."

Astrid nodded as relief fell over her. It wasn't easy for her drive to the Keys Resort. Shame seemed to tug at her more than ever.

"You have any idea what you would like to do here?"

"It doesn't matter."

Zane nodded once more. "How about I show you around? Give you more of an idea what you'll be up against? I'm hiring in all positions at the moment due to the sports season coming up. But our more solid positions are front desk/check-in, and housekeeping."

"Okay."

"We also have a gym that stays open from seven in the morning to seven in the evening. The hours are the same with the two indoor family pools unless cleaning and sanitizing is in motion," Zane explained to Astrid.

"Who cleans them?"

"All staff are required. They all rotate to share the load. Once a week."

Astrid stood beside Zane in the center of the tennis courtyard. So far, he took her on a tour through the inside of Keys Resort and through most of the outside amenities. The scenery of the hotel was more than colorful and rich, it was a serene scene and people flocked from everywhere to enjoy it.

"Looks peaceful." Astrid noted.

Zane slid his hands comfortably down inside of his pockets. "I aimed for that in my blueprints. Glorious view, and water."

Astrid used her hand as a shield over her brow and stared across the way of the Belmont Sea towards the row of boats parked along the harbor. The docks were full of people dressed in their casuals, and swimwear. Some of them with fishing poles and buckets.

Nervously, Astrid tugged at her lower lip for a moment. "Staff ever go out there?"

Zane looked in the same direction. "Sometimes," he replied. He looked back at her sympathetically. "But it's not required. Mostly during staff parties. Holiday gatherings. That's when everyone occupies the boats or just bask themselves in the air along the docks."

"How much is the starting pay?"

"Temps are eighteen an hour. Regulars are started off at 15 with both sports season and holiday bonuses."

The last thing Astrid wanted to do was be a pool cleaning girl. Or a housekeeper. Front desk rep didn't seem to meet up with her lack of desire to be social and she was certainly not in the condition to be a cook on sight. Really, what she wanted to do was sleep but that was no longer an option.

"You're capable of doing whatever you sign up for, Astrid." Zane assured her gently. "I have great dependable supervisors and staff who'll walk you along. Not to mention, I'll be here. Whatever you need."

Pulling her attention away from the harbor, Astrid stared up at Zane. She always remembered him to be a creature of perfect features but being older seemed to leave everything about him more defined. His eyes for one. The pictures she'd seen of him throughout the years were hardly close to the real-life images of him.

Focus, Astrid. You hate him, remember?

She looked towards the tennis court clubhouse centered between the massive golf field and gift shop just as a few stayers went zooming by on their golf carts. "Any positions open for the tennis house?"

"Part time mostly. If you want full-time, you'd also have to be responsible for golfing equipment being in place and available for customers. Some days require longer hours than stated, but it's not as stressful as it sounds once you get the hang of it."

Astrid nodded.

"Okay."

"You're open?"

"Yes."

"Great. We can get started on your paperwork then. I'll get Honey to give you a rundown of everything you need."

"Thank you," she mumbled, crossing her arms.

"So, now that we have that out of the way. Why don't you tell me how you've really been Astrid?"

Astrid pressed her lips together as she looked back up at him. "You've seen the news like everyone else. I'm pretty sure you have an idea."

"No. What I know is that the first time you saw me after twelve years, you ran away from me."

A sudden feeling of dread washed over Astrid. She hadn't come here to be investigated. Nor did she come to be treated like some patient in need of some evaluation.

"I wasn't expecting you," she told him bluntly.

Zane nodded. "I apologize for the inconvenience you felt. That wasn't my intention."

When he took a step towards her, Astrid squeezed her hands along the hold on her elbows. "I'm glad you're back," Zane told her.

"How can you say that?"

Zane stared down at her for a moment before completely closing in the space between them and wrapping his arms around her. The temptation to pull away, to scream and curse all bombarded Astrid at once.

Just who the hell did he think he was hugging her?

Touching her?

Most of all, why did it feel so good?

The full softness of his body.

You're grieving, Astrid.

That's the diagnosis.

Pull it together.

The emotions ping ponged through Astrid until they eventually came to rest. She inhaled, and the scent of both fresh soap and cologne filled her senses. She felt the grazing of Zane's beard brush along her neck. A gold cross necklace he wore, pressed coldly along the underlining of her chin. She fought not to close her eyes and pressed her head along his chest.

Please let go.

Please let go.

I can't handle this right now.

"The things you remember about me—that's not what it really is, Astrid." He whispered to her.

"That's how I can say that."

Pressing her hand along the plushness of his chest, Astrid leaned slightly away from Zane to stare up at him. Deja Vu hit her like a ton of bricks, and she could see the same pair of caring eyes staring down at her just as she had that night on the Swanny Merriott. To add more fire to the flame, there was something else behind them. A flicker of something that tugged and pulled at her insides like a rope tied to a bull.

"If I were to ever get a chance with Daytona, I'd make his ass regret hurting you," Zane told her huskily.

Astrid's lower lip dropped but no words would come. And even if they did, she would've been interrupted.

"Daddy!" a voice sliced between them.

Caught off guard, both Astrid and Zane broke away from each

other in an instant and turned their attention to the girl running over to them.

"No running, Sage!" Honey ordered her as she followed over in the same direction.

Rolling her eyes, the young girl halted her running and changed her pace to a brisk walk. "Daddy, I'm hungry. Ms. Honey said she would take me to midtown to get some burgers and fried onion rings, but I have to ask you first..."

"How do you know Ms. Honey doesn't have plans?"

"Because...she said she would take me. Duh."

"Don't get smart with me, Sage," Zane warned her as she approached them.

Adjusting her purse strap on her shoulder, Astrid tried her best not to stare so hard at the young girl. The task was difficult. Her mind immediately went to Ariyah and how she would never be able to see her grow as big. The girl resembled Zane in so many ways, yet she didn't all at once.

"I didn't bring you up here to bug my secretary."

"It's fine," Honey replied as she finally got close enough. "I really don't mind. She overheard me telling one of my girlfriends that I want something from Ninx Burgers."

"She's supposed to be spending time with me." Zane interjected.

"Daddy, I have the rest of the afternoon to bug you! Please let me go! Please!" Sage begged.

"I'll bring you back something!"

"Oh, you're going to buy me something with my money?"

"No. Why would I do that? Honey is paying."

Astrid watched Zane and his secretary exchange glances of amusement before he gave in.

"Fine. But before Ms. Honey heads out, she's gotta help your daddy with a future employee first," Zane told her.

All three of them seemed to be in sync when they looked at Astrid, but the one whose stare was more direct was Zane's daughter.

Astrid suddenly felt as if she were standing there with some odd hairball out of place.

"Congratulations," Honey acknowledged.

Astrid forced a welcomed smile. "Thank you."

"Do you wanna come with us?" Sage asked in the direction of Astrid.

"Ummm, no. I'm sorry. I, uh, have somewhere to be after I leave here."

"Come on," Honey smiled at her. "Let me get you plugged in."

Astrid couldn't seem to get to her car fast enough once she was done filling out paperwork for her new job. Out in the parking lot, she almost tripped over her own feet. As she reached her car, she searched frantically for her car keys inside of her purse. She was almost successful in her quest until the sound of someone calling her name made her pause. Astrid looked up, and suddenly felt as though the wind was slapped out of her at the sight of Donovan.

He sat inside of a golf cart. The expression on his face hardly welcoming. Just as Zane had changed, so had he. The handsome boyish looks Donovan once bared were exchanged for more dominant ones. But while Zane's eyes were still soft and pleasant, Donovan's eyes resembled a man who'd seen and done far too much.

"Donovan..." she spoke.

Turning off the cart, he stepped out of the cart. Donovan stared back at her sternly.

"It's...nice to see you." she told him.

"I would say the same but I think we both know I wouldn't mean that shit."

Inwardly, Astrid cringed at the harshness of his words. If she didn't feel she deserved his cold shoulder, she would have replied back with something more vulgar. She didn't expect him to have his arms wide open for her, but the hate blazing in his eyes was enough to send her running back to Daytona.

"So, you plan on working here?" Donovan went on to ask.

Astrid shifted her weight from one leg to the other. "Something like that." she replied.

"Emm," Donovan grunted. "Guess I can't say anything to that except congratulations."

"Thank you," Astrid muttered.

Donovan stared back at her a second longer as if he were trying to find something else productive to say. When he couldn't, he gave up and hopped back into the driving cart and started it up again. Before driving off, he said, "Do yourself a favor, Astrid. Try not to run away this time just in case something doesn't go your way."

Astrid watched the sand on the asphalt kick up in the air as Donovan went speeding off. She went back to looking for her keys. By the time she got them, tears were streaming down her face. Once inside of her car, she gripped the steering wheel and let out a scream that morphed into an even bigger river of tears.

I can't do this. I can't...

I can't...

Astrid cried until everything on the inside of her went weak and the only thing that could stop her was the ringing of her cellphone. She ignored the call. Leaned her head against the steering wheel. She slipped into quietness long enough to hear the rapid beating of her heart drumming on the inside of her chest.

Once again, her cell phone began ringing. Sighing, Astrid wiped at the liquid draining from her nose. She reached into her purse to retrieve her cellphone. It was Serenity.

"Hello..." she spoke as clearly as she could.

"Hey, love. Everything turned out okay?"

"Uh, yeah." Astrid replied, wiping her face. "Did you get a chance to speak with Zane?"

"Yes. I got the job."

Serenity squealed from the other side of the line, and Astrid smiled tiredly. "I knew you would. We have to go out and celebrate."

"Serenity, honestly. I'd rather just sleep."

"Of course you would. And you can do that. Just not tonight. You, my beautiful sister, will be celebrated."

"For what?"

"Surviving. That's what."

The next several weeks proved to be crucially challenging for Astrid. She often found herself in limbo between her emotions and dealing with her physical ailments while doing her best to remember work protocols and procedures at Keys Resort. The tedious process of becoming accustomed to coworkers all over again, attending to customers and company rules, constantly running into Donovan, it all seemed like a horrid movie in rotation with an ending to crash.

Still, day after day, Astrid found herself getting up and continuing to breathe. She muscled up enough courage to bathe herself again. Cook for herself. Brush her own hair long enough not to cry in between. She purchased herself a personal journal, and with every breath she took, Astrid found a page inside of that journal to mark that she wasn't dead yet.

Day 1

Dear me, Astrid Naomi Montgomery,

I am lonely for the daughter I lost, but I'm still here and I don't know why.

Day 7

Dear me, Astrid Naomi Montgomery,

I am lonely for a sister I couldn't save, but I'm still here and I don't know why.

Day 10

Dear me, Astrid Naomi Montgomery,

I am lonely for the love I thought I had, but I'm still here and I don't know why.

Day 17
Dear me, Astrid Naomi Montgomery, I still want to kill Daytona.

Day 20
Dear me, Astrid Naomi Montgomery,
I'm lonely for a love that I know doesn't exist for me.

Day 25
Dear me, Astrid Naomi Montgomery,
At eighteen years old, a man—a monster named Othello stole something from me. I've been lost ever since.

Day 28
Dear me, Astrid Naomi Montgomery,
This morning I woke up with the itch to dance. Nothing makes sense.
Nothing.
Absolutely nothing makes sense.

"Caramel Ballerina"
She moved to the rhythm of her pain, Bending to the motions
Of unstabled winds Abstract, Incoherent,
To the sounds Of peace, Of love,
Of quiet,
Instead,
She grasped to the rhythms Of storms,
Of twisters, Addicted to the quaking,
Of unhealed Memories,
Of unhealed things,
All of it,
She piled it all in her bag
Of hard knocks,
Of guilt,
Of shame,

And then, the levees, Holding together
A mass of self destruction broke,
And she was forced to see herself Naked,
Bare,
Stitched up and down, through and through, With left over scars and bruises from life
She was forced to see that she was still lovable
And very much still loved.

Under Fire
ZANE

Zane stared back at Dr. Smollett as if he saw a ghost. "Come again?" he asked.

"You heard her the first damn time?" Mia retorted. She stood up from the soft cushioned chair she and Zane were sitting on.

"Is there any form of abuse going on in your home?" Dr. Smollett repeated.

"The hell kind of question is that?" Mia inquired in a tight tone.

Reaching out for her hand, Zane tugged, motioning her to sit back down.

When Dr. Smollett called Zane earlier asking if she could meet with him, he hardly expected her to ask him anything pertaining to child abuse. What he expected was for her to possibly have already come up with some type of behavioral diagnosis that would explain Sage's erratic outbursts lately. She phoned him in the middle of one of his staff meetings with enough worry in her tone to cause grief. And considering what she was insinuating, he understood why.

Dr. Smollett adjusted her glasses by slightly pushing them up on the wide bridge of her nose. "I know this is a hard question to consider. I am not pointing fingers at either one of you."

"Sounds that way to me," Mia hissed.

"I understand, Ms. Hall," Dr. Smollett acknowledged. Her eyes darted between both her and Zane. "However, it is a very valuable question that I believe comes into play."

"What exactly gives you the idea that Sage could be getting abused by anyone?" Zane inquired.

"I've watched Sage. I've listened to her talk."

"That's what the hell we pay you to do." Mia fumed.

"Mia..." Zane said in a warning tone.

"She doesn't exactly give off the pedigree of a child with bipolar. Anger management issues, yes," Dr. Smollett continued. "However, based on our exercises, she does give off a number of symptoms of a young girl struggling with something serious."

"And you think that something is us abusing her?" Mia continued to push.

Dr. Smollett's face became burdened with lines of worry. Zane could see it. She was getting frustrated with Mia's unwillingness to understand where she was going.

Standing, Zane began pacing the floor slowly out of the sudden turning in his stomach. He couldn't fathom someone hurting his Sage. He hadn't known her as long as he should but the years he did miss, he made up for it. He and Sage had gone out just yesterday evening to a movie, and then dinner afterwards. During their bonding, she showed no hints of anger towards him.

"Mr. Keys, I know this is upsetting. But, please, just keep a clear mind on where I'm steering you. Abuse can come from anyone. Maybe at her school, perhaps? Kids around the neighborhood? A close family relative?"

Pausing in his pacing, Zane stared back at Mia who in return stared back at him bewildered.

"Why are you looking at me that way?" She frowned.

"Who have you had around our daughter, Mia?" he asked calmly.

Mia's mouth shot open. "Are you fucking kidding me right now?"

"Do I look like I'm auditioning to be a damn comedian?"

With flaring nostrils, Mia shot up from the couch and came to stand close enough to Zane for him to smell the hint of alcohol on her breath. It was masked under the aroma of green mints.

"How dare you ask me something like that?"

Zane stared back at her. He couldn't put his finger on it, but something was happening with his daughter, and she was behind it.

"Mr. Keys. Ms. Hall. May I make a suggestion?"

"Hell no!" Mia barked.

Zane looked back to the woman. "Go ahead, Dr. Smollett."

"Fine," Mia replied. "I'm not giving this bitch another second of words." she huffed. Going back over to the couch, she flopped down on it and claimed silence.

"Who does Sage spend the most time with?"

"Me!" Mia blurted.

"I thought you weren't talking anymore." Zane retorted.

Mia rolled her eyes and turned her attention to the wall once again.

"Mr. Keys," Dr. Smollett grabbed his attention again.

Zane turned to look back at her. "My apologies. Sage is mostly with her mother."

Dr. Smollett nodded. "Is there a possibility that for the next two weeks, you and Ms. Hall can come to some sort of agreement by allowing Sage to stay with you?"

"I've tried that. Mia isn't up for it."

"Maybe, just maybe, you two can talk it out for the sake of Sage." Dr. Smollett said.

"I'll do whatever needs to be done when it comes to my daughter's well being." Zane made it clear. He looked over at Mia. "Other people have to be willing to."

With a hard scowl on her face, Mia stared back at both Zane and

Dr. Smollett. "Ugh!" she groaned. "Fine!" She stood up and came to stand before them. "I will let Sage stay with you for the next two weeks. But don't you dare have anyone else around her in that playpen you call a qualified living space."

Zane reframed from responding to Mia's remark. What he needed to say wasn't for Dr. Smollett's ears.

Without so much as a thank you or a goodbye to Zane or the woman who's been professionally nurturing their daughter, Mia stormed out of the office.

"I'm very sorry, Mr. Keys." Dr. Smollett said, thoughtfully. "I'm not trying to cause any friction at the expense of you or your relationship with your daughter. But I needed to point this out before someone on the outside ends up having to intervene. Something is definitely happening with Sage, but bipolar isn't one of them."

Zane rubbed at his beard. "Dr. Smollett, you don't have anything to apologize for."

"Can I give you something?" Dr. Smollett asked before walking over to her file cabinet. She pulled out one of the drawers and removed a folder labeled with the name Sage Hall. "Yesterday, I asked your daughter to draw out two things. One, of something that gives her peace, and another, of something that terrifies her."

Dr. Smollett pulled out two sheets of paper from the folder before coming back over to Zane.

"Here," she said, handing the papers over to him. "Your daughter loves art, no doubt. But I think it is also her way of saving her own life."

Zane took in the two pictures. Both of them were labeled in Sage's handwriting. One read PEACE, and the other FEAR.

On the paper labeled PEACE, there was a picture of a boat and a woman dressed in a ballet suit dancing on the deck.

It was so detailed that it haunted Zane. All the times Sage made it known that she hated her drawings, this one was even more perfect than the one he pinned up in his office. But the part that stood out to him was the ballet dancer.

"She said she dreams about that one often," Dr. Smollett revealed with a smile.

Zane turned his attention to the picture labeled FEAR and he was both immediately perplexed and worried. It was a simple picture drawn in a grayish shaded bubble with a cigar in the center of it. There were white marks used as impressions of smoke.

"She cried the entire time she drew this one. She mentioned that she was afraid you'd hate her."

Zane took in the picture that was just as detailed as the first one. He swallowed the sudden lump in his throat. "I smoke cigars. Are you saying I'm the reason why she's acting out?"

"If I didn't see the way your daughter's face lights up when she talks about you, Mr. Keys, I would think that. I do have to be honest and say that I don't really know where she's going with this yet, but you aren't the mystery here. We'll just have to wait until whatever's plaguing her reveals itself."

Once Zane departed from Dr. Smollett's office and into the parking lot where Mia was parked beside him, he didn't dare hold back for the sake of hurting feelings.

"So, what else did she say to you?" Mia asked Zane as he approached. "I guess my character is in question now, I bet?"

Coming to stand in front of her, Zane stared back at her. "How many glasses have you had?"

"What?" Mia cocked.

"Don't play with me, Mia. You know exactly what the fuck I'm asking."

Mia scoffed. "I'm a grown ass woman, Zane! I don't have to answer you about anything!"

"If I find out you're the one behind Sage's behavior—"

"Are you seriously standing here threatening me?"

Zane stared back at her with a gaze of seriousness. "We both know I've never rolled like that, Mia. Zane is peaceful as fuck. But Z, he ain't showed his ass in a while."

Intimidation crept up on Mia's shoulder at Zane's words.

"If it's something you wanna tell me, say it now and we can hash it out." He told her. "I told you from day one, I'm willing to help you with anything. You're the mother of my daughter, Mia."

Mia huffed. "Oh, my God! I don't have anything to say, Zane!"

Momentarily, Zane nodded. "Okay," he replied, walking over to his Ferrari and getting in. He started up his engine and rolled down his window. Putting on his shades, he told Mia, "Don't say I didn't ask you. Anything I find out beyond this point is on you. Have Sage to me by one o'clock tomorrow."

Rolling up his window, Zane sped off fast enough to kick up dust into the air.

∽

"I swear," Zane said to Blaze. "Mia is the culprit in all of this. I can't put my finger on it, but she's involved."

The two men sat in the back of the Red Lace Gentlemen's club occupying one of the red velvet booths. It was a full house per usual, and Zane wasn't up for being on the scene the way he often was. He called in all of his security, and Tamaya, his self-appointed supervisor, to practically run the place while he sat back.

Along with the rest of the crowd, he watched one of the dancers, Violet, masquerade along the stage in her lace lingerie. The full-figured beauty serenaded the crowd of mostly men and a few here and there girlfriends to Maxi Priest's Close To You. Out of all of the plus size women Zane hired within the last year of opening the adult establishment, she was the most captivating.

"What do you think Mia's doing?" Blazed inquired.

"If I say it, I'll have to kill her myself."

Blaze stared back at him thoughtfully. The anger that Zane was trying to suppress was evident, but there was also something else that was doing its best to fight its way through.

"I'm pretty sure you laid that part of yourself to rest for a reason, Zane." He said logically.

"Shit was breakin' my parent's heart," Zane muttered as he took a sip from his glass of Hennessy. He recalled his days of running the streets with not a care in the world or whose heart he broke. "Our relationship is still strained but not as much."

"Sounds deeper than parents' issues." Blaze insinuated.

The words landed on Zane. He felt them. He knew exactly where Blaze was going and he didn't stop him. To own up to them outright, though, he was hesitant.

"Does this have anything to do with Gabe?" Blaze went on to ask.

Zane's eyes stayed glued to the dark liquid in his glass for a moment before looking up at him.

Sometimes, he was sure that he and Blaze were as much as brothers as him and Donovan. He'd been where Zane was in some instances and suffered dire consequences behind it. Blaze went through hell and managed to bounce back. Yet, here he was every other day questioning why he was still in place.

"I'm still not clear on what happened," Zane vented. "He was bipolar, B. But that shit wasn't why he killed himself. I can still remember the look in his eyes. There was something else that was eatin' at him. Dr. Smollett says that isn't the case with Sage, but I refuse to miss that shit."

"I hear you. You just gotta let it play out young blood." Zane nodded.

"If I'm going to be honest, I don't know where my brother's head is these days," Blaze said.

"Nigga been missing in action, and when he does show up, he's quick to haul ass."

"I'm pretty sure he has a logical reason."

Blaze smirked. "I recognize the patterns, Z. There's nothing

85

productive that my brother could be doing. But I won't be a negative Tyrone."

For a while, the men continued to drink on their beverages as the crowd in the room continued to be serenaded by one exotic dancer after the next.

"How's work?" Blaze broke the silence.

"Work is work," Zane replied nonchalantly. "Got a meeting with a construction crew in the morning. Thinking about expanding the hotel."

"I guess I should be more direct," Blaze stated. "How's Astrid?" Zane leaned back in the booth.

How was Astrid?

He spent a majority of his time trying not to watch her as often as he wanted to while she was on the clock. He damn near tripped over his own feelings the day he hired her. He got too close by hugging her, and he promised himself he wouldn't do that again. The move had taken them both by surprise, but not as much as the words he let slip from his lips about Daytona.

It was a thought that wasn't meant to be said out loud. Zane couldn't explain it. It was as if he slipped back into the mode of protecting her just as he used to.

"She's been productive." He told Blaze.

"Productive," Blaze repeated, humorously. "The tension I saw between you two that day we went to Daytona, I meant to bring it up sooner. But I at least wanted everything to cool down before I did."

"We're old associates. You know that already and everything else Serenity filled you in on."

"I wouldn't classify a man constantly reaching out to a woman he used to know as just an old associate."

"Where are you going with this, B?"

"You're a lonely ass man with a god-hero complex, Zane."

"The God-hero complex is to be debated. Maybe. But ain't a

damn thing about me lonely," Zane refuted. "I have choices. You're standing on one of my main picking grounds."

"I'm not talking about some brainless hookup," Blaze replied looking over Zane's shoulder.

"But since you have such a hefty picking ground as you state, you should be more than welcoming at your choice for tonight my brotha." he pointed.

Zane followed Blaze's finger towards the entrance door where his wife, Serenity, and Astrid stood.

The lust that swelled in the pool of Zane's eyes was undeniable. The sight of Astrid lured him in right away. He wasn't sure what part hit him first. He concluded it was the seductive way she filled out the strapless, honey colored dress she wore. It stopped mid-thigh with a finishing split. Open toed glass heels grace her feet, putting an arch in her back distinguished enough to make his mouth water. Her locs hung freely, and her lips, full, were cherry red.

"Control yourself, young buck." Blaze told him with a wide grin as he stood. He winked slyly at Zane before making his way across the room to meet the women.

Zane forced himself to stay put. He inhaled at the sudden heat clouding around him. Tugged at the sudden tightness of his shirt. He wasn't surprised at Serenity showing up. Every once in a while she got an erotic itch that involved her being a lady of the night for Blaze. In doing so, she would dress up in her own exotic dancer's get-up and occupy one of the private rooms to give him a show. Had he known Astrid would eventually start joining her on her nights out, he would've mentally prepared himself.

From where he sat, Zane watched as Blaze exchanged kisses with Serenity and then planted one on Astrid's cheek. He whispered something in her ear before pointing in his direction. Astrid's eyes followed, and for a second, she locked in on him before breaking eye contact. Zane could see the sudden discomfort in her. She wanted to run back out of the club but she couldn't. That would make her look like a sore thumb.

Eventually, Serenity and Blaze stepped away for a moment and Astrid was left to stand alone. She looked over in Zane's direction again and then back to the stage where another dancer was grabbing the attention of the room.

A pinch of amusement weighed on Zane. There was something about the sight of a woman trying her best not to appear anxious. In Astrid's case, it was sexy as hell. She scooped her river of locs to one side of her shoulder. Nibbled nervously at her lower lip. Gripped her elbows and did her best not to appear to be as awkward as she obviously felt. The view did nothing but fuel the fire suddenly burning on the inside of Zane at the sight of her.

Standing up, he swiftly made his way over.

"You like it?" Zane asked from behind her.

Astrid turned to look up at him. "What?"

"My club. Do you like it?"

"It's...a club."

"Sure, it's a club. But do you like what type of club it is?"

Astrid frowned. "What kind of question is that?"

"It's a valid one."

Sighing, Astrid turned her attention back to the scene before her.

"You look beautiful." Zane complimented.

"Mhmm."

"A thank you usually follows after a compliment."

"Would that make you feel better as a man if I did?"

Zane smirked. "I'm pretty sure the compliment itself definitely made you feel better as a woman."

Shaking her head, Astrid muttered something out of annoyance. She hadn't changed at all.

Zane leaned in closer to her. "Same Astrid Montgomery," he remarked. "Let me reiterate my statement for you. You look beautiful, but you also look awkward as hell standing here when all you have to do is come over to the table and sit down."

Astrid peered back up at him. "You looked occupied. I didn't want to distract you."

That time, Zane shot her a look of annoyance. "Stop playin' yourself, Astrid," he told her before walking away and back over to the booth.

Claiming his seat again, Zane focused his attention back on the stage. At least he tried to. The here and there sips he took from his beverage gave him plausible reason to continue looking over in Astrid's direction. He didn't have to spy on her for long though. Eventually, she gave in and came over.

At first, she stared back at him as though she was waiting for him to tell her what to do next before giving in and sliding into the booth.

Zane stretched an arm along the top of the booth seat. "You can come closer than that," he told her. "I don't plan on doing anything you don't want."

Hesitantly, Astrid slid closer to him. As she did so, Zane caught the sweet aroma of cocoa butter, vanilla, and soap. "Thirsty?" he asked.

Astrid rubbed at her arm. "No. Already had a few shots before getting here."

"Astrid, you don't need to be uptight around me. We've practically seen each other every day for the last several weeks."

Astrid raised a critical eyebrow. "It's not every day that I'm sitting inside of a strip club."

"Would it make you feel better if we got a more private room?"

"Is that your way of trying to insinuate something else?"

Grabbing her hand, Zane gently squeezed it. "Astrid, chill. What I'm saying is that I have plenty of rooms here that don't involve seeing things that may make you uncomfortable."

Pursing her lips, Astrid slowly removed her hand from underneath his. "I'm fine." she dismissed.

Nodding, Zane turned his attention back to the stage once again. He tried his best not to be bothered by the closeness of the creature beside him. The smell of her. The feel of her hair grazing along his arm. Her skin.

"I've been meaning to tell you," he spoke again, "You've been doing great at the tennis club house. Tamya's been keeping me updated on your progress."

Astrid pushed a smile. "Yes. I saw her at the door. Thanks."

"How do you feel about it so far?"

Astrid looked at him. Blinked her eyes in a way that made her lashes flutter, sending shivers through Zane.

"It's different."

"Do you feel safe?"

"Safe?" Astrid repeated.

"Yes," Zane nodded. "Do you feel like you can come and go as you please without the pressure of anyone invading you?"

"I'm pretty sure it doesn't matter. It's a job."

"It matters, Astrid," Zane told her. "Just like it also matters that it's been a while since anyone's asked you that. Or that you would rather deflect an honest question with sarcasm to hide what you really want to say."

Astrid stared back at him without blinking at that time. She was caught off guard and Zane was almost at the breaking point to gloat about it. "You're obviously the master conversationalist. Just how many women do you say that line to?" Astrid asked smartly.

Zane narrowed his eyes. He fought at the charismatic grin tugging at his lips, but it was impossible. "Look around. I've had practice."

"Yeah, I bet."

"Mhmm."

Astrid shifted around a bit inside of the booth. She was uncomfortable, but it wasn't the type of discomfort that required Zane to give her space. It was the type of discomfort that came when a woman found herself in fire she didn't intend to feel.

Zane inhaled as he drank in the erotic shapes of her features. He found his attention glued to the delicate landscape of her collarbone. He gulped.

Damn she's beautiful, he thought.

Pull yourself together Zane.

"Zane," someone called out.

Breaking his attention away from Astrid, Zane looked over at Tamya. "Sorry to interrupt you two," she said, "But I need to speak with you."

The temptation to deny her request was strong, but Zane didn't go that route. The urgency in her tone alerted him that wouldn't be a wise choice.

In the far back of the club, Zane and Tamya stood inside of his office.

"One of the security guards saw a woman dressed in a red hoodie taping this to the window of your car," Tamya said. She held out a piece of paper to Zane folded in two. "They tried to stop her, but it was too late. Baby girl was quick."

Zane stared back at Tamya for a moment. He prayed this wasn't yet another illegitimate baby that he didn't know about. Apart from the latest hookup, he really had slowed down, and he'd learned the meaning of never being too safe with protection. Taking the paper, he opened it up and read the words perfectly written in pen.

Dear Mr. Keys,

Please, meet me at this address alone by midnight. 1745 Carrington Lane. It's about your daughter, Sage.

P.S. He's hurting her, and Mia knows!

At first glance, the words seemed to be a blur. As if they were running lazily into each other. Zane wasn't sure if he read right. What he was sure of was the sudden rapid thumping of his heart inside of his chest. The fire that went shooting through his veins.

. . .

"I can have Vashty run the cameras back in the parking lot, but I doubt it'll do any good." Tamya told him.

Zane continued to stare at the piece of paper. "What did she look like?"

"Brown skinned woman, full figured with curly shoulder length hair and one hell of a sprint," Tamya described. "She did have a limp. Before she saw us that is."

Folding the paper back in two, Zane squeezed it in his hand and tucked it into his pocket.

"Run the cameras back," he ordered Tamya. "Hit me up and tell me if you find anything else."

"Are you going to meet her?"

"Yes," Zane replied as he turned to leave the office.

In the hallway, Zane retrieved his cell phone from his pocket and called up Donovan.

"Yo," Donovan answered.

"D, we got problems."

"Where are you?"

"Red Lace."

"Alright. I'm about to make my last drop for Binx. I'll be there in fifteen."

Back out onto the main club floor, Zane returned to the booth. The seemingly cool, calm posterior he sported was shifted to a tensed one, and Astrid noticed.

"Um, is everything okay?" She asked.

Zane didn't reply. He rubbed at his beard in an effort to calm the storm brewing on the inside of him.

"Should I go?" Astrid spoke once more.

Zane looked at her with a gaze that was harsh enough to cut through ice. The glossiness of his eyes caused her to pull back an inch.

When Astrid stood up, Zane reached out to grab her hand. He didn't respond. Not because he didn't want to. His words were lost.

Hesitantly, Astrid slid back into the booth. She watched as Zane dropped his head. He rubbed at a spot on the back of his neck in an effort to fight the tears that stung at his eyes from the fire boiling on the inside of him.

"Zane..." Astrid said to him in a more concerned tone.

When he felt the gentleness of her hand on his arm, Zane lifted his head to stare at her again.

"If I asked you to come with me tonight, would you?" he asked her.

Astrid's face became flushed with both confusion and temptation.

"It's about my daughter," Zane verified.

Slowly, Astrid dropped her hand. "Your daughter? Is she okay?"

"No."

Standing up, Zane reached out his hand to her and Astrid stared at it. She was hesitant, uncertainty masking her face.

Placing his hands on the table, Zane leaned into her close enough for her locs to graze the side of his face as he brought his lips to her ear.

"My apologies for invading your space back in Daytona. My presence was requested. Now the tables are turned. I'm not asking you to come with me because you owe me something. After all of these years, I still don't feel that you do. I'm asking you because I feel like you understand what I'm feeling right now."

The words were direct. Full of honesty. Vulnerable. Pulling away, Astrid looked up at him. Her intrusive honey eyes searched Zane's face as if she were trying to find error in him. She didn't. Astrid stood. "Where are we going?" She asked.

Reaching into his pocket, Zane handed the paper to her for her to read. The same level of emotion grew on her face only it was more sympathetic than anger.

"Where is Sage?" she inquired.

"With her mother. But before I make any sudden moves, I need to find out what this is about." Momentarily, Astrid nodded.

"Okay." She replied in a settled tone.

Grabbing her hand, Zane led the way towards one of the rooms in the back where Blaze and Serenity were.

Heatwave
ASTRID

Sitting alongside Zane in his Ferrari was the last place Astrid expected to be. Her night started out as a girl's outing at her and Serenity's usual spot, The Deluxe 500 lounge, along with Serenity's best friend, Nahvea.

However, midway through the evening, Nahvea got an emergency phone call from her job and Serenity received a personal call of her own from Blaze that was really disguised as a booty call. Considering the nature of everyone's dismissal, the two strawberry margaritas and three shots she consumed altogether, Astrid made up her mind to call it a night. It was Serenity who wouldn't hear of it. The moment they pulled up to Red Lace, Astrid immediately caught on to why and by then it was too late.

Now she was sitting in the passenger seat of a drop top as headlights zoomed past like lasers while the wind played twirlies with her locs. She and Zane cruised down Quentin Avenue. The scent of his car mingled with the exhaust fumes filling the night air, new leather and violet incense. But the most prevalent scent was him. His cologne and aftershave engulfed her space. Tugged at a part of her brain that sent shock waves to areas of her body she was sure had died away long ago.

Maybe it's the alcohol, she thought. *It has to be the alcohol.*

Astrid peered over at him as they came to a stop light. Zane's jaw was clenched tight. He tapped along the steering wheel impatiently that told of inward anticipation. The night formed around his large silhouette in the most masculine way. When he looked over at her, she felt herself almost cave in at the weight of his gaze.

Damn. He's fine.

Much easier to look at than Daytona's ever been. Much easier than any other man— Snap out of it, Astrid.

You're only here for support.

"Sorry for the speed," He said. His voice dropped an octave since they left the club.

Astrid didn't respond. Instead, she looked at the time displayed on the dashboard. It was ten minutes past midnight, and they had twelve more minutes to go before they reached Carrington Street. They left the gentleman's club thirty minutes ahead of time, but the nightlife traffic caught them.

"I'm sure you don't have anything to worry about," she said.

"I don't feel that." Zane replied.

Astrid didn't argue. Who was she to tell anyone how to feel when it came to the well-being of their child when guilt still had her in a chokehold? Or the fact that some days she wasn't sure if she was coming or going.

"Your daughter," she said. "How old is she?"

"Twelve going on twenty-five."

Nodding, Astrid smiled delicately. She could only imagine how beautiful Ariyah would've been. "You should do everything you can to make sure she's protected. She expects that from you."

Zane stared back at her. His features, firmly set in the most upfront and sexually intrusive way. A few complex lines formed along his forehead and creased around his mouth. Astrid was unaware, but her skin glistened. Her vision blurred, and she thought maybe it was the alcohol. Her eyes became a pair of watery pools, turning her vision into glassy doubles of everything. When Zane reached out to wipe at a lonesome tear that went rolling down her cheek like a fallen star out of space, she was alerted. Astrid leaned away.

She hurried to wipe at the next set of tears attempting to follow suit. "Sorry," she mumbled.

"Nothing to apologize for," Zane told her.

He stared at her long enough for the light before them to shift to green. The car behind them beeped their horn. Like a ready speed racer, Zane sped off down the rest of the way. It was twenty-five minutes past midnight by the time they reached their destination.

"Shit looks like a set up to me," Donovan remarked as he stepped out of his ride.

"It looks abandoned," Serenity added.

"Damn right it does, baby," Blaze agreed.

"But the only thing left for Zane to do is go inside. Whoever the woman is, she knows Sage and Mia well enough to leave him a note about them."

Zane and his men, along with Serenity, all stood outside of the house marked 1745 on Carrington Street. Partial darkness flooded the neighborhood, but it was the full moon and a few spacey surrounding houses that managed to give some type of life. The house before them, however, looked as if it'd been vacant for months.

"Looks more like a hide out," Zane observed.

"In that case, you don't need to go in alone." Blaze pointed out.

Zane shook his head. "I'm not." He told him as he stole a look in the direction of his car.

A few feet away, still sitting inside of his Ferrari parked along the curb, Astrid continued to do her best to gather herself. Zane let up the top to give her as much privacy as she needed. She managed to clear up her emotions for the rest of the drive to their destination, but the moment they pulled onto Carrington Street and Astrid saw Donovan, everything hit her like a ton of bricks again. It was as if she were suddenly sucked into a time warp and back on the Swanny Merriott.

Pulling down the mirror visor, Astrid took in her reflection. Luckily, most of her mascara was still in place. It was her foundation that needed repairing. She decided just as quickly that she had no choice. Reaching for her purse on the car floor between her feet, she removed her small container of makeup wipes and began removing her foundation and any other remnants of makeup until her skin was bare. Once she was done, she took a deep breath before finally stepping out of the car.

All eyes were suddenly on her. Particularly Donovan. Astrid looked over at him. Read through the disdain at her presence just as she had that day in the parking lot.

Looking away, Donovan leaned along the hood of his car and crossed his arms.

"You okay, sweetie?" Serenity asked.

Astrid forced a welcome enough smile. "Fine," she replied. She looked at Zane who still looked tense, but the complex lines in his face had softened up a bit. "I...didn't mean to make you wait," she told him.

Zane shook his head. "Nah," he replied. "Trust me, I needed a breather. I don't know what the hell we walkin' into?"

"You takin' her witchu?" Donovan spoke.

Astrid looked back over at him, his expression even far more disapproving. "If you would like to go inside with him. That's fine too."

"No," Zane interjected. "It's alright."

Astrid watched the two men exchange looks, and eventually, Donovan backed down.

"Whateva' man," he blew off. "Like I said. Ten fuckin' minutes. Anything longer than that, I'm comin' ready to blast."

Before making their way towards the house, Zane reached out his hand for Astrid and she grabbed it.

When Zane knocked on the door, no one answered. It was Astrid who led the way to turn the doorknob, discovering that it was unlocked. As they entered, darkness hit them for the first few steps, but there was a faint light from a fireplace giving view to a mildly spacey living room.

Closing the door behind them, Astrid suddenly felt eerie. The aroma of burned smoke, and old dust filled their nostrils. From where they stood, the house appeared to be destitute but there was a faint sound of a television on low volume coming from another part of the house.

"Hello!" Zane called out. "Yo! Is anybody here?"

They both waited for someone to say something back, but there was nothing. "We need light," Astrid whispered.

"Hold on," Zane whispered back. He released her hand for a second before taking a few steps forward into the spilling darkness.

He hadn't let go for long, but for Astrid in that moment, it felt entirely too long. "Zane," she called out to him.

"Hold on, baby," he replied back.

The sound of his voice, the reassurance, sent an unusual wave of peace to fall over Astrid as the sound of a light switch flickered back and forth filled her ears. Reaching out her hand, she felt her way along the wall and plastered herself to it. When the faint sound of a light switch came again, she inhaled with relief as she and Zane were finally surrounded by light.

Astrid met eyes with Zane standing nearby the fireplace. "You good?" he asked. Astrid nodded as she walked over to him.

They took in the state of the room in which they stood. On the outside, it looked very much destitute. The space in which they stood, however, resembled a neatly sophisticated room that was hardly touched.

"I get the feeling this woman has a low tolerance level for

anything being out of place," Astrid noted.

"Low tolerance is hardly the word." Zane mused.

Astrid's attention landed on the fireplace. Walking over to it, she inhaled the fresh smell of burned wood. Someone had been there not long before they arrived. From the specs of paper dust, they were burning something other than just wood itself. A companion set was propped along the side of the fireplace, and she was drawn to reach for the fire poker that hung from it.

It was the feeling of Zane's hand on her back that paused her.

"Nah," he said. "Shit is neat in here. Too neat. Don't touch it."

As much as Astrid wanted to go against the moral code of common sense, she thought better of it and pulled her hand back.

She tugged thoughtfully at her lower lip. She was suddenly just as lost as Zane. Why come to someone about supposed vital information on their family's well-being if you weren't going to be in place? The feeling of uneasiness settled in her stomach. Something was wrong, but not to the degree of their safety.

She looked towards the opened door of a bedroom where the sound of a television came from. When she took a step to walk in that direction, Zane gently tugged her back by her wrist.

"What's up?" he asked.

"Something's wrong," she said.

"If you feel like that's the case then you need to stay by me."

"No." Astrid shook her head. "I don't think we have anything to worry about. At least, not directly."

Zane stared back at her in a complex manner.

"Didn't you say she ran off?"

"Yeah. That's what Tamya told me."

"If she had something to tell you, why didn't she just come inside of your club and do that?"

"Obviously she didn't want anybody to see her."

"But why?" Astrid stressed. "Who was she worried about?"

Zane tossed around the question in his head. Astrid could see it.

He was trying his best to understand where she was going, but it was foggy.

"There's a possibility that she wanted your help, Zane." she said.

"For what?"

"She knew something you needed to know which she made very clear. But maybe she wanted you to..."

Astrid gasped when it hit her. She looked back over towards the open door of the bedroom. "I think we need to call the police," she said.

"On what? All I got is a note to go off of. They'll say anybody could have written it."

Grabbing his hand, Astrid led Zane to the bedroom. Upon entering, just like the living room, there was nothing that appeared to be out of place until Astrid dropped her attention down to the carpeted floor. "Zane." She grabbed her hands along his shirt and tugged without pulling her gaze away.

Zane followed her attention downwards. "Shit," he muttered.

There were spatters of red stains—blood, that trailed the floor. They both followed the trail of stains that led towards the cracked bathroom door. The sound of dripping water caused Astrid to have heart palpitations.

Walking over, she shoved the door open. "Oh my god!" Astrid gasped at the sight of a woman slumped over naked in the bathtub. Her neck was slashed, and a bullet was lodged into her brain.

Looking back up at Zane, Astrid could see the flashbacks rolling in the pool of his eyes as he stood frozen at the horrid sight. She reached up to palm her hands along his face. "Zane!" she attempted to snap him back. "Zane! Look at me!"

Blinking, Zane looked at her, his eyes shadowed with tears. "We have to call the police! Now!"

"Yo, what the fuck!" Donovan's voice sliced in between them.

Both Astrid and Zane turned to stare back at him standing in the doorway, Blaze and Serenity behind him.

Erotic Propositions
ASTRID

"You'd be surprised how many fine ass rich men we meet on this field," Daphne carried on. "And their wives don't give a damn. As long as their checks don't stop."

"My, my, my. Now that's got to be the most foul thing I've ever heard you say today, Daphne." Tamya replied. "There are far too many men in the dating pool for me to choose to be fooled by one."

"I'll believe that when you stop screwing your ex-husband."

Standing alongside her two extremely coherent coworkers, Astrid stared aimlessly out into the golf field of the Keys Resort in which they stood on. As usual, during the afternoon hours, they were collecting scattered golf balls and other miscellaneous trash strewn about the field. At least that's what they were supposed to be doing. They still had more than enough sections to inspect and clear.

On a normal day, Astrid would be more than aggravated with the lack of dragging time out on work chores. She wouldn't speak on it. She would keep her grievances to herself because she adapted to her coworkers becoming so easily distracted at times.

Daphne was always to blame, and her good Judy, Tamya, wasn't in the business of chastising her for it. Bottom line, both women had an itch to birdwatch.

Out on the furthest parts of the golf field were a group of men who just exited out of the men's locker rooms with their golfing equipment in tow. According to Tamya, this set consisted of lawyers, tv entertainers and brokers who took vacations very often at the Keys Resort. They were also a sight for sore eyes according to Daphne.

Astrid found that piece to be debatable. But even if she were interested, she couldn't focus.

For three days she'd been this way. Out of tune. Out of touch. And it had everything to do with the dead woman she and Zane found 72 hours ago. Her name was Layla Brooks, and apparently, she and Zane shared a one-night stand not long ago. But that bit of information was the least of their worries.

The policemen were called as Astrid suggested. The dreary scene turned from just her and the rest of the crew being there to the policemen, detectives and a slew of CSI's being present. They swept the deceased woman's house from top to bottom. They found nothing in the search at first. Then a photograph of Sage turned up. And just as they were about to give up on discovering anything else, one of the CSI's found a half-burned note tucked inside of the fireplace. Most of the words were burned away but half of the notes still held a very important message.

The words HE'S AFTER ASTRID MONTGOMERY TOO were written in capital letters. Astrid hadn't felt like she was able to breathe much since.

"Astrid," Tamya's voice snapped her back into the present.

Blinking, Astrid looked at her.

"Damn." Tamya cocked an eyebrow. "You just drifted off to the deep end huh?"

Astrid exhaled tiredly as she tugged at the snugged cleaning gloves on her hands. "Didn't get much sleep," she said. "Insomnia."

"Mhmm. I've been there." Tamya padded her shoulder. "I was

saying that Daphne swears she knows which one of those dogs out there has the most bones."

Astrid waved her hand in dismissal. "I'm pretty sure they're focused on more important obligations," he replied in an attempt to divert the useless conversation.

"Girl, please!" Daphne disputed. "Like what?"

"Their cars!" Tamya cackled.

"More like how long they can stay away from their wives while their girlfriends are driving their cars."

"I swear to you ladies," Tamya planted her hand on her chest dramatically. "One of those brothas who's name I'll refrain from mentioning, brought his other woman to my home spa last weekend. Spent over four hundred dollars on her. The week before, his wife got over a thousand dollars' worth of beauty treatment."

"Relationships definitely have a new meaning these days," Daphne said.

"Tuh, you got that right." Tamya cocked.

"Ladies!" One of the men yelled out to them. He was tall, pretty boyish, and he sported a millionaire smile a mile long. "Beautiful day, isn't it?"

While Daphne and Tamya waved and exchanged greetings back like a couple of schoolgirls, Astrid crossed her arms militantly. There was no man captivating enough to catch her attention. The number of male customers who attempted to talk to her since day one, she hadn't kept count. She didn't care. She knew what they wanted, and she wasn't willing to give it. Sitting inside of Zane's Ferrari almost left her to question her own sanity, but that wore off. She hadn't seen him since that night, and it was fine by her.

"See him." Tamya placed her hand on Astrid's shoulder as she pointed over to the same pretty faced man. "That's Mr. March. He's the owner of that big fancy Zanders store for women over on Gaithersburg Way in midtown. He has ten other store locations and a black card to match."

"And how do you know all of this?" Astrid asked.

Tamya smiled deviously. "I'm the only female worker at the Red Lace. Let's just say we run in the same circles."

"How convenient," Astrid replied.

"Very."

Astrid adjusted the sun visor she sported. "When you ladies get done groveling at the married golfers, we need to sanitize this equipment."

"Ohh, Astrid." Daphne frowned. "We're single women who work on a vacation spot away from home. Practically paradise. You may as well catch a few nuts."

"No thank you." Astrid mumbled.

"You're better than me. If it ain't the golfers, it's that damn Mr. Keys. I swear, I'd pay for him to have his way with me."

Astrid didn't reply, but as Tamya stole a secretive glare at her, she looked away. She knew what the look was for. She saw far too much that night inside the Red Lace.

Her co-workers continued to bask in conversation at the sight of the golfers until one of them took it upon themselves to wave them over. Astrid ignored the invitation and carried on with her work duties until she grew tired enough to take a seat inside of the cart. There, she watched Daphne and Tamya from afar juice the charm out of the golfers for everything it was worth.

It was the buzzing of her cellphone in her pocket that pulled Astrid's attention away from the soap opera. Removing it from her pocket, she saw that it was both her sisters, Trina and Sky. She'd yet to speak to any of her family since she returned home. They were aware she was there. Serenity made sure of that. The phone calls had come back-to-back. Astrid knew what to expect, and because she did, she decided she wasn't ready.

Still, she read the messages anyway.

Sky: Grandma and Grandpa miss you.

Trina: Just how long do you plan on dodging us? We're your sisters Astrid! Sky: We love you! You don't have to deal with this alone!

Trina: Yes we love you! I swear, Astrid! I'm going to hunt you down if it's the last thing I do! We're only keeping our distance out of respect for continuously hassling Serenity.

Sky: Stop it, Trina!

Sky: Astrid, please call us!

Astrid's eyes watered at the display of the messages. It was the shame of it all. Her daughter was dead because she didn't have the guts to leave a man she loved. A man whom she was sure would've eventually killed her. The regret that tore at Astrid caused her to stay away from her family. She could still hear the memories from a past she'd rather forget.

"You lost your scholarship for what?" Sky had fumed at her. *"Because you couldn't handle a damn rejection?"*

"Did you even think about what we would've done without you had that monster gone any further? Trina added.

"I did not raise you with the mindset to throw away your life!" Darina, her grandmother, cried.

Her grandfather, Abraham, had nothing to say, but Astrid could still recall the sadness in his eyes. The only one who'd stuck up for her, was Blu.

"Ms. Robinson," Zane's voice came bursting through the cart's transceiver.

Sliding her cellphone back down into her pocket, Astrid stared back at the device. She sat frozen long enough for Zane's voice to come again.

"Tamya," he said more directly. "You there?"

Adjusting herself, Astrid removed the handle of the receiver and pressed the response button.

"This is Astrid," she muttered.

"Ms. Montgomery," Zane corrected in a more conscious tone. "Good morning."

"Morning..."

"Is Ms. Robinson near you by any chance?"

Astrid looked back out towards the field. "Uhh, she's..."

Come on, think of something, Astrid thought. She rattled her fingers along the steering wheel.

"Hello?" Zane's voice came back in.

Astrid pressed the button again. "Umm, she's assisting a few customers with some questions out on the field at the moment."

"I see," he replied. "Would these customers happen to have a name? Mr. March perhaps?"

Damn it.

"Dodging the question won't help, Ms. Montgomery." Zane pressed.

"Uhh. I'm not aware of his name."

"Are you lying to me?"

Astrid rolled her eyes. "No."

For a moment, silence settled between Astrid and the transceiver. She looked back out at the field in time to catch Mr. March lean into Tamya and place a kiss on her cheek before whispering something in her ear.

"Ohh, come on, Tamya," Astrid groaned in disdain. "Hurry up. Both of you."

"Astrid," Zane's voice burst through in static. Her heart thumped inconsistently at the sudden personal way he said her name.

"Yes?" She answered hoarsely.

"When you get the chance, come see me."

Sighing, Astrid replied. "Yes sir."

Hanging up the speaker, Astrid delivered a few curses to the air. Surely she wasn't about to get fired already. If she were, she was most definitely going to light into both Tamya and Daphne.

Starting up the cart, Astrid pressed her foot to pedal and zoomed back to the clubhouse. Once there, she placed the bag of golf balls in the back stock room for sanitation. She grabbed one of the clubhouse keys before going to exit doors, but she couldn't get past them before gasping at the sudden sharp pain that went shooting through her stomach. She gripped her hand along the check-in counter and forced herself to pull it together by breathing in and out.

Come on, Astrid.

You took your medication already.

Just pull it together.

She hadn't felt the pain in almost two weeks which was a giant improvement. But at the moment, it was making up for its time lost. She clenched her hands tightly along the counter for a full ten minutes until the pain passed.

"Have a seat," Zane told Astrid as she entered his office.

Sitting down, Astrid watched him as he opened the drawer to his desk and pulled out a cigar and a lighter. He lit it and put it to his lips before walking over to the large window and staring out of it as if he were trying to gather his thoughts.

Why was he doing this to her?

Torturing her.

If he wanted to fire her for lying, why did he have to make it so dramatic?

Or better yet, why didn't he just say that he thinks it's best that he let her go because too much has taken place?

Sucking in air, Astrid stood back up. "If you're going to fire me, just do it."

Pulling his attention away from the view before him, Zane stared at her perplexed. "Say what?"

"Isn't that why you called me up here?"

"No, Astrid. It isn't."

Astrid pressed her lips together and rubbed awkwardly at her elbows.

"I already know how Tamya rolls. Her and Daphne. But they're great employees. They know not to go too far within the confounds of my establishment. This is not about them."

Astrid sat back down. "Oh?"

"I have a proposal for you. But before I get to that, Detective Reid and Detective Grant came to see me yesterday. They want to talk to us both sometime tomorrow."

Astrid grunted. "I don't have anything more to say," she said. "I don't know Layla."

"We're in the same boat here in some ways, Astrid. Neither of us know her but she knows us."

"I'm pretty sure you're more familiar than me."

Zane stared back at her as though he wanted to refute her statement. He didn't. Instead, he came closer to her and leaned along the edge of his desk. "To be transparent here, I've spent these last few days trying to figure out whose place we were at the night I did see Layla up until yesterday. According to the detectives, she had two places of residence. But the one on Carrington Lane was a designated hideout. They just can't connect who she was hiding from."

"Well, none of that helps my end."

"Are you saying that you don't want to talk to them?"

"I'm saying I don't have anything to say." Astrid replied tiredly. "Just in case you forgot, I came down here to escape from being in the public."

"No. You came down here to face what you've been running from for the last twelve years."

Astrid scoffed. "Okay. Can we get off of this subject? Please. My answer is no."

Blowing smoke from his lips, Zane nodded. "Onto the real reason why I called you here," he said. "My secretary, Honey, will be out of town for the next four weeks. Her father is sick. To make sure she isn't missing out, I'm giving her some time off. I'll need someone to take her place until then. I thought you'd make a good fit."

Astrid tossed around the idea. She had no plans of working so closely with Zane. His hotel was full of other female workers. Why did he feel like she was a good choice?

A string of smoke went lingering around her and Astrid looked back at him staring back at her. There was a sudden flutter inside of her stomach at the sight of him holding the cigar to his lips. She adjusted herself in the chair she sat in at the uncomfortable feeling. "I'm...not sure if I'll be as good as her."

"I'm not looking for you to be. Answering phones, booking appointments, meeting sit-ins, and assisting me on a few local business adventures. Those would be your duties. Most of it isn't anything you haven't done before."

"Right."

Astrid stood up and walked over to the window. She took in the overview of the Belmont Sea. The sun shining down on the water made everything look serene. It was the sight of the boats that made her feel uneasy.

As if he could read her mind, Zane said, "No boats will be involved. Rules still haven't changed from the day I hired you."

"Is this your way of showing some type of favoritism because I don't need it."

"Astrid, it's not that type of proposition."

She turned and looked back at him.

"Then why me?" She asked. "You have other workers who've been here far longer than I have."

"True. But I want you."

The words were innocent, but the way they fell from his lips, Astrid felt as if she were sucker punched with a feeling of...something she couldn't identify. It was an unexpected flutter that swam through her body. It was the same magnetic pull she felt the day he gave her a tour around the resort. The night inside of the Red Lace. The Ferrari. It wrapped itself around her and with all its might, reeled her in. As if those unorganized feelings weren't enough, Zane came to stand close enough to tower over her like a beautiful brown shadow.

"I know I've already said this," he told her. "But you'll be safe. I can guarantee you that."

Astrid took a small step back. "I'm not worried," she told him.

"I don't believe that."

"You're free to believe whatever you want." She stated defensively.

The urge to put up her guard was evident. If she didn't, there was a possibility that Zane would mishandle her like every other man. He would prey on the obvious vulnerability that tended to sneak up on her.

"I'm almost sure that if you hadn't been in that house with me, I would've done something stupid," he said.

Astrid frowned. "Like what?"

"Like trying to revive a dead woman," Zane revealed. "All I saw was Gabe, Astrid. Layla's blood would've been all on my hands. Literally."

Astrid tried to fight the sudden sadness that washed over her at Zane's boldness to be transparent once again, but it was tough. She saw something she hadn't seen since the day she began working. Fear. Anger. Broken heart. "I'm glad you decided not to."

"Yeah, but if something else pops off. I'm not sure if I'll be able to handle it. At least not alone. Which brings me to my next favor in question," he said.

"And that is?"

Rubbing at his beard, Zane took a few steps back away from her. "I would like for you to come stay with me."

Immobile, Astrid stared back at him. The silence that barricaded itself between them was piercing. "Stay with you?"

"I know this is a bit forward," he went on to say. "But it's not what you think. I figured since Blaze and Serenity will be out of town for the next four days, why not come stay with me?"

"Who told you they were gone?" Astrid inquired skittishly. The question was dumb. And she quickly shook her head. "Never mind that." She blew off. Yes. Serenity and Blaze were on another one of their business ventures, but she was doing fine. Even with everything that took place, mentally, she was getting by. "Is this what you think I owe you?"

"I don't think you owe me anything, Astrid."

"Hmmp. Tell that to my sister. I'm pretty sure Donovan feels the same too. The hero who rescued the stupid girl who went and got herself raped all because her best friend didn't want her back. Fast forward to now and I'm still the woman who needs rescuing. Except now a dead body is involved."

"Is that how you see yourself?" Astrid sucked in an air of frustration.

"Astrid, what happened to you the night of our senior trip, it wasn't your fault."

"Can we not do this? I will be your secretary until Honey gets back. But this? Staying with you? No." Astrid made clear before turning to leave the office.

She needed to clear out before she was triggered. She could feel the next episode coming. But just as it happened in the clubhouse, her plan to exit was derailed. The sharp pain went riding through Astrid's womb like a lightning bolt. Gasping, she halted in her steps at the searing pressure.

Come on, Astrid.

Just make it to the door.

Then go hide in the bathroom.

Or your car.

Or somewhere more logical than your own boss's office who's already seen you in more unflattering ways than you've wanted.

When she felt Zane's hand along her back, Astrid took another step, and the bolt of pain struck her again. She wanted to run but her body wouldn't allow it.

"Astrid," he said.

"I'm fine." She told him in a broken whisper.

"No, you're not."

Astrid attempted to take another step, but it was Zane gently gripping her back by her elbows that prevented her. He circled an arm around her waist, tugging her back against his chest.

"Breathe, Astrid," he told her.

Shame enveloped her. She wanted to find somewhere, anywhere to hide as the repetitive bolts went surging through her. And then, there was the warm feeling of Zane's hand gliding along the hold of her belly. Gently, he pressed there.

"The tumor," he said. "Is this where it hurts you?" He found a spot where the lump was and held his hand in place. "Astrid, talk to me," he urged her.

Slowly, Astrid nodded. "Yes." She replied, on the brink of tears.

"Close your eyes," he told her.

"What?" she asked frantically.

"Close them."

Astrid wanted to reject his order. What the hell was he going to do? What the hell was closing her eyes going to do? She'd tried that. In fact, she would do just that if she could get away and find herself a safe space. It was the voice inside of her that scolded her pride, causing her to give in. Slowly, Astrid shut her eyes.

"I need you to breathe in," Zane whispered to her.

Astrid felt his lips brush along her ear. With a single tear falling down her cheek, she inhaled deeply.

"Good job," Zane affirmed. "Breathe out." Astrid exhaled.

"Do it again." He ordered.

Once more, Astrid did as she was told. She inhaled slowly, and then exhaled. Zane quoted the technique to her over and over until she felt the pain cease. Until the only thing that existed was the weight of shame and silence.

Shielding her hands over her face, Astrid fought to hold in the rest of her tears. This wasn't supposed to happen.

"It's okay," Zane assured her. "Let it out."

He came around to face her before she could protest and took her into the hold of his arms. A wave of emotion washed through Astrid as she clung to the large man before her. She buried herself in him like a scared girl in a cave. Inhaled his scent.

Astrid, what are you doing?
Let go, she told herself.
Do yourself a favor and let go now!

Astrid sought to pull away, but Zane held onto her. Her hands, clenched into fists, slowly opened. She pressed them along his soft chest where she felt the erratic beating of his heart.

"If you wanna know the other real reason why I chose you," Zane whispered. "I've been missing my brother a lot lately," he confessed. "I've felt for a while that you would be the only one who understands what I'm feeling. You can imagine trying to get to the bottom of how to save your own sibling only to realize it's a waste because there are no answers that will leave you settled."

The words struck Astrid in a personal way. She was guilty of that very thing. Losing Blu was one of the biggest mysteries to her that she had no control over. Now she had her baby girl to add onto it. She balled her hands into Zane's shirt. "I don't think I can help with that."

"Considering that you're still here is helping more than you know."

Slowly, Astrid raised her head. Her face, wet with tears. She stared up into a pair of gentle brown eyes, and the urge to hide herself in them gripped her. She tugged nervously at her bottom lip. "Um, I need to go," she said, pulling herself out of his hold.

"You don't have to leave." Zane told her.

Astrid shook her head. People change in life. She was the ultimate example. But someone like Zane, it stood out as highly unlikely. "We've always hated each other."

"I've never hated you, Astrid."

"Bull shit," she disputed. "Shall we go down memory lane?"

Zane cocked his head to the side in a nonchalant manner. "What you remember is not what is," he told her. "But I won't stop you."

"You always did your best to let me know you never cared for me being around."

"What you remember is me looking out for you without you even realizing it."

"No. The Zane I remember was a rude ass gangster who thrived off screwing every fast ass airhead around the neighborhood he could get his hands on!"

Zane cocked an eyebrow. "I don't deny that, baby. But you would make this much easier on your emotions if you just admit that you wanted to be one of them."

Astrid gasped. "You wish! You're still the same arrogant, egotistical asshole!"

"If that's how you feel then why are you standing here trying to fight your feelings for me?"

Astrid became flushed. Her eyes watered again as she tried desperately to find her words. Heat consumed her. Relentlessly, it hovered over her. The hesitation to explain herself left her wide open. And before she could react, Zane reached out to cup her face in his hand. He gently grazed his thumb along the fullness of her lips as he closed in the space between them.

"You're having a hard ass time believing me because you think I want to take control of you. I don't. At least not in the way that you think. I've never hated you, Astrid." Zane emphasized once more. "I was in love with you. If I couldn't have who I wanted, why would I try to have anything serious with anyone?"

It wasn't an actual question Astrid needed to answer, but she almost did. Had Zane not pressed his lips to hers, she would have.

Gathering her into his arms, Zane delivered a kiss to Astrid so deep it felt as though the floor beneath her had fallen away. The kiss gave way to rivers of submissive moans she didn't know existed within her. It felt as though the blood in her hands were rushing and she could feel her own heartbeat in them. But the heart thumping, the heavy breathing and moans didn't belong to just her. Some belonged to Zane. She had no idea how she got here. In a place so deep that she had no strength to get out.

The weight of everything that took place in Astrid's life, it rang so loudly. She had to break free. She needed to before she became too far lost.

Astrid felt Zane's large hand roam to the center of her uniform skirt. She moaned against his lips as he cupped the soft center between her legs.

Breaking the kiss, he looked down at her. "Tell me what you want me to do," He whispered. Astrid stared up at him void of words, but the glazing passion in her eyes gave her away. Zane read what she wanted; what she needed.

Moving his hand up, he tugged at the opening of her skirt, the entrance of her panties, and slowly slid his fingers down south into the warmness of her nest. Astrid gasped at the feel of his touch. He hadn't removed his other arm from around her, but she gripped her hands along the desk for balance anyway.

"Mhmm," Zane moaned deeply. "Relax."

Astrid swallowed hard. Her breathing was hollow. Her mind was locked in, but she was fighting her hardest to hold on to herself.

"Astrid," Zane whispered to her once more. "Relax," he told her again.

Leaning her head back, Astrid closed her eyes and succumbed to the magic of Zane's hand, his fingers awakening her. Everything around her disappeared as he rubbed at her delicate center. A wave of ecstasy engulfed her, and she was suddenly swallowed up. Snatched up into orbit. The cry from her lips started as a small alarm, telling the story of an erotic release building up. She became weak at the rocking strokes of his fingers.

Slow.

Steady.

Brilliant in the motion.

"That's it baby," Zane affirmed huskily.

When he began to speed up, Astrid's breathing quickened. She clenched her hands tighter along the edge of the desk. She was suddenly spinning. The sound that built up in her throat, she didn't recognize. No man had ever found a spot deep enough to produce a pleasure to this magnitude.

It was music to Zane's ears.

Pressing his lips to hers again, he swallowed the gigantic moan that was due to burst from her lips. He kissed her until the bolts that went surging through her crashed and everything went silent.

"Emm," Astrid groaned. She pressed her hand to Zane's chest. "Please," she begged breathlessly. "Stop."

Immediately, Zane did just that. He stopped. He removed his hand from her skirt. He stopped kissing her. But he didn't back off. He brushed his lips along her cheek. Slowly trailed a path of heat to her ear where he pressed his lips there, sending new electric bolts up her spin. "You plan on making this difficult for the both of us, it can be that way. Playing cat and mouse is my forte," he whispered to her. "Or you can just let me continue to help us forget everything that's gone wrong in both of our lives."

"That's what you're used to. Women being at your mercy." Astrid attempted to argue.

"No, Astrid." Zane said looking into her eyes. "In your case and in your case only, I'd be at your mercy."

With labored breathing, Astrid shoved Zane away and stormed out of the office.

Outside in the hallway, she tucked away a few locs that came out of place. Did her best to gather herself. Zane had placed his mark on her, and she didn't want it to stop.

The Other Side of a Coin
ZANE

"Your offer is more than pleasing to my ears, Mr. Keys. You'd be surprised how some of these businesses show their appreciation by trying to low ball me and my crew with bogus compensation. Guess they can smell new blood."

"Yeah, they can. You and your men won't have to worry about that here."

"Great. We can start working immediately."

Standing to his feet, Zane shook hands with Jordan Kyle of Kyle Construction & Labor. He officially closed the deal on having him and his construction crew come work on adding new amenities to the resort.

"You won't be disappointed. Wednesday morning," Mr. Kyle quoted. "Six o'clock sharp?"

"Sounds good."

As Zane saw Mr. Kyle out of his office, he was met with Detective Reid and Detective Grant standing along the hallway wall. "Detectives," he acknowledged.

Detective Reid raised an eyebrow. "You're free now?" he asked.

"Lucky for you and your partner, yes." Zane replied nonchalantly.

Entering back into his office, the detectives followed him in.

"Will Ms. Montgomery be joining us?" Detective Grant questioned, closing the door behind them.

"No," Zane replied. "She's in training."

"She's going to have to speak with us sooner or later,"

Facing the men, Zane crossed his arms like a bodyguard. "Well, it won't be today." Both men nodded.

"How's it been for you?" Detective Reid investigated. "Yow know, since our last meeting?"

"How do you think it's been for me?"

"Mr. Keys, we're not here to allude to anything pertaining to Layla when it comes to you." Detective Grant assured. "Other than what you've shared with us, you're still in the clear."

"Seems that way."

"Maybe so. But obviously, there's a deeper connection here than you thought."

Zane stared back at the men. For the last four days, his mind went over any possibility that could link his daughter to the likes of Layla. He was drained at this point. Walking over to his desk, he sat down. "I just need to know one thing," he said. "Is someone after my daughter?"

"That's what we're unclear on." Detective Grant answered.

"What is there to be unclear about?"

"We haven't found any other source as to why Layla had a picture of your daughter. However, I do have a thoughtful question. Who is around her on a daily basis? And is there anyone you feel could be of harm to her?"

Zane's mind immediately went to Mia. Sage was still with him. Surprisingly, her mother let her stay longer because of the dramatic decrease in her behavior. However, there'd been an unexpected thorn in the bush. Mia finally admitted that she indeed had a drinking problem. But while Zane was more than warm to the idea of his daughter being with him, Mia was hardly off of the hook with him.

"It's not going to be of benefit to you or your daughter to protect anyone," Detective Reid said. "No matter who they are."

"There isn't a soul on this earth that's more important than the safety of my daughter," Zane made clear in a hard tone. "Sage has been with me. When she's not in school, I come to pick her up. If I can't make it, my secretary does."

Detective Grant stuffed his hands in his pockets. "So she stays with her mother most of the time?"

"Yes."

"Why isn't she with her now? We spoke with Ms. Hall and she claimed it was best for the moment."

"Yes. She agreed to let our daughter spend more time with me."

"Why?" Detective Reid grilled.

Zane rowed his shoulders out of sudden agitation. "Detective Reid, we both know women. They don't trust us until they need to."

"Right. So why does she suddenly need to?"

"I just told you. Sage needs more time with me."

"You're choosing this to be a circus with no doors, Mr. Keys."

"The hell does that mean?"

"What are you not saying?"

"Look, if this is how you two plan on going about our meetups—you wanna grill me for some shit you think I know, both of you may as well dismiss yourselves."

Detective Reid scratched his forehead tiredly. "We're trying to help you here, Mr. Keys. There's a dead body and your daughter's life is involved. Should we start to question your involvement now?"

"You fellas are free to do whatever you want. I got too much going. No woman is worth throwing it away for."

With a stone face, Detective Grant reached into his pocket and pulled out a quarter. He tossed it on Zane's desk like some professional money peddler. "There are two sides to a coin, Mr. Keys. You gotta choose which side you want to land on."

"I'm choosing my daughter's side. You or nobody else is coming between that. I got her."

"Damn it. Someone is framing you, Zane." Detective Grant emphasized. "I've seen this before. If you let this ride out how you're doing, Sage won't have a father to come back to."

Zane didn't reply. He could see where this conversation was going, and if he wanted to continue being the honest man he promised himself he would be, he knew it was wise to end it.

Standing, he walked over to the door, and showed the two detectives out without a word.

They have no idea how far I'll go for mine, he thought. *No idea at all.*

"Daddy," Sage's voice broke into Zane's thoughts.

He peeled his eyes away from the school of white ducks flapping their wings along the water banks and looked over at his daughter. She sat across from him with a frown, vanilla ice cream smudged along her chin from her vanilla and strawberry sundae. They'd been sitting outside at Crestview Park for about an hour, but his mind was elsewhere.

Layla.

The detectives.

The erotic confrontation with Astrid.

"I'm talking to you," Sage said maturely. "Where are you?" she asked.

Zane reached out to wipe the ice cream from her chin. "I'm here, baby girl."

"It doesn't seem like it."

"Daddy apologizes." He forced a smile. "What's up?"

Sage perked up. "I was asking, are you coming to my class presentation next month?"

"What presentation?"

"It's a science project my teacher Ms. Celestine assigned to us. I built an entire plant system from straws, Styrofoam balls and cups. It started off a bit amateur, but it turned out great. I won second place."

Zane smiled genuinely that time. "That's genius, little mama."

"Thank you. Ms. Celestine said I gotta tell the class how I came up with it. You know, the ins and outs and stuff."

"I'll be there."

"Great," Sage replied. "Mama said she may come. It depends on her hours at work."

"I'm sure she'll make it too."

Sage shrugged. "Doesn't matter if she doesn't."

Zane watched his daughter as she adjusted herself in her seat. The excitement on her face became partially dimmed with sadness. "Have you drawn any more pictures lately?" he asked, diverting the conversation.

"No," she replied glumly. "I mean, the last one was Ms. Astrid."

"You drew a picture of her?"

Sage nodded. She reached over for her book bag on the ground underneath the table and pulled out her art book. Opening it, she placed it before Zane.

Zane took in the picture of Astrid dressed in ballet attire. Immediately, he was snatched back in time during his years at Camden High. He'd skip class to go to hers and watch her rehearse for upcoming recitals just to clear out before she would notice him. The picture before him depicted parts of those moments.

Astrid's hands were raised in proper ballet form as she stood on the tip of her toes. The most eye-catching feature was the sea water background that resembled the harbor at the resort and the swollenness of her belly. Her eyes were closed, and she was smiling. The picture was just as perfect as the one hanging up in his office, and far deeper than the two Dr. Smollett kept on file.

Zane stared so hard he almost lost himself within the drawing lines. As if he could see her moving along the page.

"When did you do this?" He mumbled.

"A couple weeks ago," Sage replied. "She's pretty. And she's nice. Strange, but nice. Is it true? Did she really lose her baby?"

Looking up, Zane stared back at Sage thoughtfully. "Yea,"

"That's tough," she replied sadly. "That would make me strange too."

Zane looked down at the picture once more. He navigated his attention to the page number scribbled at the bottom corner, number 77. "Just how many pictures have you drawn like this?"

"A dozen. I kept dreaming about it. Before it just used to come and go with no face or color. Then I met Ms. Astrid, and I realized it was her."

Zane frowned. "Come again."

"I dream about her. It's no big deal. I dream about everyone. You. Mama. Ms. Serenity…"

"Sage, you haven't known Ms. Astrid long. The picture in my office is over several months old."

Sage shrugged carelessly before shoving her spoon into her dessert and taking a bite.

Zane wanted to further elaborate as to what was happening, but he stopped himself. There was a possibility that Sage wouldn't understand or become fearful all together.

"And anyway," Sage went on, "I'm thinking about giving that a rest."

"Art? Sage, you love art."

"Not anymore."

"Since when?"

Looking up from her dessert, Sage stared back at him in the most discomforting way before dropping her eyes back to her treat again.

Zane reached out to grab his daughter's hand. "You know I would never let anyone hurt you right?"

"Mhmm."

"Sage, look at me."

Slowly, Sage raised her eyes.

"What's up?" Zane investigated. "Why have you been raising hell with your mother? Why don't you want to draw anymore?"

Sage stared back at her father. For a second, there was a glimmer of hope in her confiding in him. A wall breaking down. But just as quickly as it came, it disappeared. Something shifted, and fury became present. "I don't want to talk about this!" Sage raged. She shot up to her feet with her fists clenched to her sides. "It's not like you would give a damn!"

Zane stood. "Sage, I'd kill to protect you."

"Bull!" Sage spat.

"What is this about? Is it because I wasn't there for you for the first seven years? Is it that I work too much? You don't feel like I spend enough time with you? What?"

The feeling was Deja Vu. Zane was sure if his daughter was holding a gun, she'd put it to her temple just as Gabe had.

Sage clenched her fists even tighter. She'd gone so far as to square up with Zane by inching in closer.

"You wanna lash out at me?" Zane challenged. "That's fine! But I'm going to keep pushing back until you tell me what the hell is eating at you!"

Clenching her teeth together, Sage let out a growl of frustration that echoed throughout the park. It was loud enough to catch the eyes of other distant park attenders. "You're not there when it's happening to me?"

"When what happens Sage?"

Sage stared up at him before crumbling where she stood. "Just please...don't make me go back..." she whispered. She dropped her head into her hands.

Reaching out, Zane wrapped his daughter into his embrace. "Is it Mia? Is she hurting you? Is she allowing someone to hurt you?" he asked.

Sage didn't answer. She didn't have to. It was the way she squeezed her arms around him, buried her face and cried into him. As if she were pleading through her tears.

"Okay, baby girl," Zane settled. "I got you."

Within the solitude of their space, for another thirty minutes Sage cried until she was empty. By the time they gathered up their belongings, she was yawning and gathered herself in the backseat of her father's Ferrari.

While she slept, Zane did his best to contain the anger blazing on the inside of him.

The number of scenarios playing through Zane's mind was endless. After seeing Sage was safely tucked away in her bed, he occupied himself in the hammock on his screened in porch. The night air rested on him just as humbly as his thoughts. At fifteen minutes past midnight, he was unable to sleep and the Hennessy he consumed did little to comfort him. His thoughts wore on him until he could do nothing but stare up at the porch ceiling fan above him.

How foul was Mia really?

That was the most relevant question.

He didn't give a damn who was screwing her. Who was hurting his daughter?

And how long had it been happening?

He wasn't in the business of forcing Sage to talk. From the look in her eyes, he knew. He'd seen it before. Astrid wore it the night he discovered her. Someone had done something foul to Sage, and Mia was behind it.

Keep your eyes on the snakes around you, he recalled Gabe's voice.

He missed what was transpiring with his own twin brother.

He missed what happened to Astrid.

Now it was Sage.

Sucking in air, Zane rubbed at the swollenness of his eyes. He removed himself from the hold of the hammock and went back into his bedroom to retrieve his cellphone. As he dialed up the numbers, he prepared himself to be ignored.

"Hello," Astrid answered in a sleepy tone.

Zane parted his lips to talk, but he choked up. His emotions were suddenly colliding and holding him hostage.

"Hello," Astrid spoke again more clearly.

Walking back out onto the screened porch, Zane took a seat in one of the soft cushioned porch chairs.

"Zane?"

"Yeah." There was a brief pause, and nothing except brief static for a moment. "Are you there?" Zane asked huskily.

"Yes." Astrid confirmed. "It's...past midnight."

"I know," Zane mumbled. "I'm sorry." He told her. He rubbed away a tear that went streaming along the bridge of his nose and dripped onto the ground.

Astrid cleared her throat. "Is there something wrong?"

Zane inhaled and closed his eyes. "Does it bother you?"

"Does what bother me?"

"That you weren't able to save Ariyah?"

He knew the question was intrusive, but he needed to know that he wasn't alone.

Astrid sighed tiredly. "Why would you call me up this late and ask me something like that?"

"Because I think it needs to be asked."

"Does it bother you that you couldn't save Gabe?"

"Every fucking day, Astrid."

Once again, silence took hold of the phone line. "It's not your fault," Astrid spoke again.

"And it's not yours either."

"Zane—"

"Do you blame me?" He interjected. "I mean, someone violates you and you have to live with the shit. You gotta figure out how to carry it and in most cases, it leads you to more fucked up situations."

"Zane, are you drunk?"

Zane pinched at the bridge of his nose from the feeling of inflammation in his nostrils. He rubbed lazily at his forehead. "Nah, not heavily. I mean, I—can you just answer me please?"

"No. I don't blame you."

"I was protecting you. You don't have to believe me, but I need you to hear it. Jarold Dixon, and Keagan Williams, they were both assholes Astrid. And Donovan, we both know how he got down."

"The same way you did?"

"Regardless, Astrid. I've always cared no matter what..."

"Thank you."

Leaning back in the chair, Zane stared up at the ceiling once again.

"Are you okay?" Astrid asked.

"Honestly, no," Zane replied. "I feel real fucked up right now." He explained bluntly. He tossed around the next question in his head. He knew what the answer might be, but he didn't shy away from it. "Can you come over?"

Silence filled the phone line again. But eventually, Astrid gave her answer. "Okay."

Smoke

ASTRID

Astrid reasoned that she was out of her mind for getting out of her bed at midnight to drive to the East side of Saxton. She was convinced as she got dressed, brushed her teeth and slipped on her running shoes that she had lost it. She went about packing her sleeping bag, but the urge to call Serenity was strong.

"You're a grown ass woman, Astrid." She told herself. "Get it together."

It didn't hit her until she was parked in front of Zane's place that she was merely running away.

The truth was, before Zane called her, Astrid was trapped in a nightmare with Othello. He was chasing her. He had eyes like Daytona, and the constant shift in his features made her feel as though she were in the twilight zone. While snarling for Astrid to come back to him, Othello's features morphed into every man she ever loved throughout the years until it landed on Donovan. Astrid had run as fast as she could from him until her desperate escape led her to Carrington and inside the bedroom of Layla's house.

She stood in the doorway watching the figure of a man carry

Layla's naked body into the bathroom and place her in the tub full of water.

"*She's next you know,*" the stranger said. "*Sage is next.*"

When the stranger pulled out his gun, Astrid gasped, alerting the stranger to turn around and face her. Her first thought was that it was Zane, but there were different features between him and his twin brother that she'd taken into account. Apart from the absence of tattoos, there was the slight angle of his nose.

The tone of his voice.

It was Gabe.

"*I'm sorry, Astrid.*" He cried. "*I'm so sorry I played a part in hurting you.*"

When Gabe raised the gun to aim it at his temple, Astrid screamed frantically until she felt the ground beneath her fall away and her body get sucked down into a dark hole. It was the ringing of her cell that brought her back to reality. She sat up in the bed quick enough to feel a pain in her neck, her face drenched in sweat.

Astrid cut off her engine. She took in the luxurious estate before her. The front door opened, and Zane stepped out. The sight of him, his husky frame dominant underneath the midnight sky, caused her breath to catch. He sported a white under shirt and black sweats.

I promised that I was done with men, she thought.

She convinced herself that she was only there for moral support. Opening her door, Astrid stepped out.

"Hey," she spoke.

Zane stared back at her before closing in the space between them. Swiftly, he swept her up in an embrace. "Thank you for coming." He whispered.

For the next two hours, Zane shared parts of himself with Astrid until he had nothing else left to give. He revealed his concern about Sage's wellbeing. Bared the guilt that rode him about Gabe's death. Uncovered the anger he felt at Mia and the confusion of everything else that was unraveling.

"When I find out who violated her," Zane expressed. "I can't promise I won't retaliate."

"You would have every right to."

"She didn't say it, but it was the look she gave me."

"Like someone had taken advantage of her." Astrid puzzled.

Zane stared back at her sympathetically. "I never forgot that look on you."

Astrid refrained from responding. She masked the excuse of her awkward quietness with the action of taking a sip of the tea Zane brewed for them.

"What's your story these days?" he asked.

Astrid placed her mug down on the table. "You already know it. Half the world does."

"No," Zane disputed softly. "They know an illusion."

"I didn't come here to talk about myself."

"What did you come here for then?"

"You called me."

"And you answered. You could've ignored me. Better yet, you could've told me no when I asked you to come here. You didn't."

Sucking in air, Astrid looked off into the night sky, but Zane wouldn't hear of her dodging him. He reached out to cup her chin in his hand, signaling her to look at him.

"You're so beautiful when you're weak," he told her. "You breaking down is not some cautionary sign for me. Don't you get it, Astrid? You're luring me in without even trying."

Astrid swallowed. Her cheeks became heated. Zane searched her eyes before leaning in to kiss her. Against her lips, his felt like warm Lillie's. She pressed her palms along his chest and did her best not to lose her balance like she'd done in his office that day.

"Zane..." Astrid whispered. "I didn't come here for this."

"I beg to differ."

"I can't go back down this road again. I've gone through hell and still am."

"What if I told you I'm willing to help you carry that?"

"Men don't carry anything except their dicks and egos."

"No, baby. That's just the ones you've chosen to deal with."

"And I suppose Othello is on that list?"

Zane's eyes softened. "Astrid, you know that's not what I mean."

Feeling herself becoming overwhelmed, Astrid pulled away. Why was he so sure of himself? So sure of her? So willing to be what she never experienced? As if he just knew that somewhere along the way she was going to give in. But then he posed the oddest question.

"What if I wanna help you heal?" Zane inquired.

Looking at him again, Astrid stared speechlessly at him. Heal? She didn't even know what that meant. It felt good as hell, but she was lost.

"What if we heal together?" He added.

"I don't know…what that means."

"I can show you better than I can tell you." He replied.

Astrid took in the intensity of Zane's eyes. It was enough for her to start to grow weak again. "I need to go to bed. We have a busy day tomorrow."

"You work directly for me. You can get started on your day whenever you want to," Zane pointed out. "But I'll let you slide with that one. I have an extra room you can sleep in. Unless you want me to hold you."

Astrid tugged at her lower lip nervously as she stood. "I'll take the extra room."

By the time they turned in, the sun was due over the horizon in the next three hours.

In a bedroom far down the hall, Astrid lay with her back facing the door. As sleep slowly found her, she didn't hear the bedroom door open. Or feel the opposite side of the bed she was sleeping in become weighted down. What she felt was the comforting closeness of Zane's body. Gently, he slid his arm along her belly and pulled himself into her. She opened her eyes partially as she felt the grazing of his nose tuck into the dip of her neck.

"Do you have episodes during the night?" he asked.

"Sometimes,"

"I'll be here if you do." He assured her.

Rolling over on her back, Astrid looked at Zane. The light of the moon shining through the window in the far corner of the room radiated around his face in the most beautiful way.

"What's up?" Zane inquired deeply. "Talk to me."

Astrid felt her stomach tighten. She wanted to cry, and she knew why. "I had a dream about Othello." she whispered. "I miss my baby. I should've left Daytona, and I didn't."

"It's not your fault, Astrid." Zane told her. He stroked a finger along the plushness of her lips.

"You gotta let it go."

Astrid moaned as Zane leaned in to kiss her. She felt herself break into a million pieces as his tongue expertly explored her mouth. Tasting the fibers of her tongue. She wanted it to last. She prayed at that moment that it would as he rolled over and positioned himself over her, but her prayers were shot down when she felt the painful tide approaching. It started off mild and then crashed like a train falling off the tracks. Astrid pressed her hand to her stomach and gasped at the sharp pain that went riding through her womb. "Emm," she shoved Zane away.

"Are you having an attack?" he asked critically.

"Yes," Astrid replied weakly. With all of the strength she had, she rolled out of bed and stood. "Please leave," she told him in a tone of panic.

"Astrid, I'm not leaving." Zane told her sternly as he stood up.

Astrid covered her face as the pain went riddling through her. Before she could slip down to the floor, Zane caught her in his arms.

"I got you," he told her.

In short, shuddered breaths, Astrid breathed as Zane slowly lowered her to the floor. It was the presence of him that caused her to hyperventilate. It was happening. He was seeing her in a compromising position yet again.

"Please," Astrid cried. She covered her hands over her face once more, but Zane denied her request not to be seen.

Gently, he grabbed her wrists and slowly removed her hands away from her face. Deja Vu hit Astrid as she stared up at him. The same pair of eyes that stared down at her that night on the swanny were staring down at her. They were full of things, deep things. Regret. Pain. Hurt. Sadness. Loneliness. Love?

Palming his hand along her face, Zane told her, "Breathe slow, baby. Just like you did that day inside of my office. Can you do that?"

Hesitantly, Astrid nodded. She forced herself to inhale and exhale at a slower pace. And as she did so, Zane reached down to slowly lift her shirt and delicately rub his hand along her stomach. He closed his eyes. "Breath in." He ordered her.

Astrid did so.

"Breathe out," he told her.

Again, Astrid did as instructed. Her breathing was rugged and labored, but nonetheless she was abiding. "What are you doing?" she asked in a strained tone.

"Praying for you," Zane replied. "Helping you heal," he added.

For the next few passing moments, the only sounds to be heard was Astrid as she continued to breathe in and out. She groaned as the last pocket of pain went streaking through her body, and suddenly, everything on the inside of her went numb.

Zane opened his eyes and looked down at her again. When he went to position himself between her legs, Astrid gasped. "Zane...?"

Zane placed a finger against her lips in gentle protest. "Shh..." He hushed her. He slid an arm underneath her, urging her to slightly arch her back belly up. Leaning in, he pressed his lips along the area of the lump. "You gotta let it go." He whispered. "The rape. Othello. Ariyah. Daytona. You gotta let it go, Astrid." he urged her.

Time seemed to disappear. It seemed like forever that they laid that way. Body to body. Zane's face to Astrid's belly. Astrid's hand pressed delicately to his face.

Everything that happened in her life within the timespan of Camden High up until that moment played out in her head. The rape. Othello. The different faces of men all disguised as him.

Daytona. The death of her daughter. It all came crashing down on Astrid. It was the sound of her crying that broke the silence. The sound of it, built up, dispersed from her throat. It was the exact sound Zane was waiting for.

Removing his arm from underneath her, he leaned down into her and kissed her, hushing the cries that spilled from her lips.

At that moment, Astrid was alerted that the line between her and Zane was crossed in a way that she never experienced with a man before. He kissed her, and she fell deep into the feel, the smell and the touch of him. It felt more than good because she wanted it. She needed it.

For the next two months, Astrid found herself spending more time around Zane than she planned. Due to the unexpected decline in her father's health, Honey requested more time off. Zane obliged her by granting her request. But while Astrid was more than understanding of her situation, she wished for the sake of her heart that she would return.

She was never supposed to fall so deep for Zane Keys. She was never supposed to find comfort in having Sage around her as though she were a replacement for Ariyah.

However, she did just that. She fell in deep and was doing her best every day to think of ways to pull herself out. She failed consistently, and the reasons, even the ones she wasn't aware of, were valid.

～

Astrid scrubbed uselessly at the water spots that dripped onto the newspaper she held. Looking up, she caught Sage's eye just as she blew a school of bubbles in her direction. One of them landed on her nose and burst.

"Sage," she frowned casually. "Come on, now. I'm trying to look through the ads."

"Bubbles are good luck. Maybe you'll find something big like my daddy's hotel."

"Unless I plan on taking in half of the families in Saxton, that won't work."

Sage giggled warmly, and Astrid did her best not to become sentimental. It was summertime, and as of last week, Sage was on break. The gap gave the two even more time together, and Astrid regretted none of it. For the last two hours, they'd sat outside at Belvedere.

"Here you go ladies," A waitress approached their table and placed two lemonade twists loaded with limitless lemons down on the table along with two straws. "Your food will be out shortly." She assured them.

"Thank you," Astrid replied.

Removing the paper wrap from her straw, she took a sip of her drink, and immediately sucked in her lips like a seahorse.

"It's good, isn't it?" Sage grinned wide eyed.

"It's bitter, Sage." Astrid frowned. "Why would you want this?" She inquired.

When they put in their order for lunch, two charcoal grilled burgers, and fried onion rings, Sage managed to talk Astrid into ordering a lemonade twist with extra lemons at the bottom because apparently it added flavor.

"It's good, Ms. Astrid!" Sage exclaimed. "Just let it settle for a moment. The flavor is coming."

Astrid grunted. "I'll wait for it." She said, "But for future references, I prefer my flavor to be right away and not delayed."

Sage giggled once more before taking another long sip of her beverage.

Shaking her head, Astrid shifted her attention back to the paper before her. She turned four more pages before coming across Sable Condominiums. When she saw the advertised prices were close within her financial means, she picked up her ink pin, and circled it.

"You should get this," Sage said, pointing at a massive building on the opposite page.

"Sage, that's a mansion. Not an apartment or a condominium."

Sage shrugged. "So. Just tell the owner that my daddy is your boyfriend and he'll buy it from you."

As much as Astrid tried her best not to laugh, she couldn't help it. "Your daddy and I are only friends."

"I'm twelve, Ms. Astrid. Not two. I'll be thirteen next month so that makes me older."

"Well pardon me, twelve and a half and not two. You're still a child. Which means you shouldn't speak on adult matters."

Sage pouted. "But I am an adult, Ms. Astrid. A little one but an adult."

"Okay," Astrid settled. "You're a little adult. Who's very smart and far too observant. Trust me, Sage. Stick to being that for now. You have plenty of time to be nosey. When you get older you can go be a spy for the government if you want."

Sage placed her hands on her hips. "I'm already a spy. And I spy that you like my daddy." she sassed.

Pressing her lips together, Astrid dropped the pen and sat back in her chair. She refrained from entertaining Sage's humor. She was a preteen. A very inquisitive one who had a habit of talking out of her head sometimes.

Or maybe she's just calling it how she sees it.

Astrid peered out towards the harbor where she spotted Zane and Mia talking along the deck walkway. Neither of them had friendly faces as they bickered back and forth.

The day after she spent the night at Zane's house, he filed for full custody of Sage. Needless to say, Mia showed no remorse in her reactions. She'd shown up almost every day just to make it known that she wasn't happy about it. But as much as she displayed a displeasure in Zane's boldness, she'd yet to come get Sage.

Astrid found Mia's anger to be both displaced and dramatic. She only picked her time to battle Zane during his work hours. Any other time outside of that, she was hardly around to fight on behalf of Sage. The entire saga was strange to her.

Rolling up the newspaper she was looking in, Astrid peered over at Sage who'd busied herself with a crossword book.

"Why don't I tell the waitress to have our food brought to the pool area? You can go and get your bathing suit."

"But you don't like water?"

Astrid frowned. "I don't have to get in," she said. "And who told you I don't like water?"

Sage gave the expression that she'd said too much.

"Damn, you really are a spy," Astrid retorted.

"No." Sage stood. "I just know you don't like water, Ms. Astrid."

"Go get your bathing suit from Ms. Honey's office. I'll meet you out at the pool?"

Nodding, Sage gathered her things and made her way back into the hotel through Belvedere.

Standing up, Astrid went about clearing off the table.

"Guess Zane's gone and gotten himself into some sticky shit, huh?"

Astrid looked up at Donovan. "I guess so," she replied.

Surprisingly, for the last couple of weeks, he'd been more social. The interactions were awkward. Mostly because she waited for the insults and dreary sarcasm. She convinced herself that maybe he was finally tired of being angry with her.

"Ain't no woman ever had me that bent," Donovan cocked as he went to stand along the railing. "You'd think we were on a live episode of Maury. The Keys Resort Edition."

Astrid grunted. "I'm sure they'll get it figured out."

"Nah. A broad like Mia. Ain't no figuring it out. Where there's smoke, there's fire. Chick is going to do some foul shit. Watch what I tell you."

Astrid reasoned Donovan wasn't far from the truth. Over the course of weeks, Mia displayed complete erratic behavior. On one hand, she understood. No woman wanted their motherhood compromised. Still, for a woman so wounded, she stayed away from Sage as if she were a plague.

The two watched Zane and Mia continue to bicker until Mia finally gave up and walked away.

She cursed her way off the harbor deck and out of sight.

"Damn right," Donovan marveled. "Made her ass walk away. I can imagine how this court drama will go down."

"Doubt she'll make it nice." Astrid mumbled. "But who am I to judge?"

"I'll say you have good enough reins. At this point Sage belongs to you."

Astrid stared back at Donovan. "That's the nicest thing you've said to me since I've been here." she mused. "I guess I'll take that. But Mia is still her mother."

"Yeah," Donovan smirked. "Alright."

Astrid continued to clean up the table. When she'd mostly gathered everything, she looked back up to see Donovan still staring at her. Something was on his mind, and she was sure that he was thinking something illicitly rude to say.

Hooking the bag on her shoulder, Astrid told him, "Whatever's on your mind, Donovan, just say it. You're dressed in your golf getup so I'm sure you'll want to make it quick."

Donovan scratched strategically at the hair on his chin. "I'm willing to drop this war between us. I was opposed at first. But obviously, my disapproval ain't no match for Zane's feelings for you."

"You had no reason to be opposed to anything."

"We were best friends, Astrid," Donovan said seriously. "From middle school on out, and you ended it in less than five minutes. Stop me when I'm wrong."

Astrid acknowledged his words. She never took into consideration how her absence made him feel. "Things were complicated at that time. I just wanted to get away."

"Yeah, well. You did that."

"I'm sorry Donovan."

Donovan stared back at her for a moment, and then held out his hand. "I accept." Astrid took his hand.

"I will admit though," he said. "If I could go back in time, I would've told you yes."

"Things happen for a reason."

"Bet that,"

Astrid wasn't aware of it at first. The way Donovan made circular motions along the top of her hand with his thumb. Eventually, she looked down as he gently squeezed her hand.

"Technically," he cocked. "You and Z aren't a couple yet, right?"

Looking up, Astrid stared back at him slightly confused. She chuckled nervously before taking her hand back.

Stuffing his hands in his pocket, Donovan laughed deeply as he turned to walk away. "Tell Z don't take too long," he blurted. "Time's ticking."

As much as Astrid wanted to find Donovan's remark as amusing as he did, she couldn't. Something prevented her from doing so. She felt a trigger on the inside of her belly. The feeling was eerie.

Later that evening, Astrid sat outside on the screened porch of

Zane's estate. She was fingering her way through a Zora Neal Hurston book when she heard the doorbell ring. She was expecting Serenity. According to the conversation they shared earlier, Astrid needed to meet Zane at his club. Serenity wouldn't dare give up the mystery of why, but the feeling made Astrid feel warm in ways she wasn't accustomed to.

Placing the book down, she looked out at Sage in the yard jumping rope with her mini radio blasting before going into the house.

As she approached the front door, Astrid looked through the peephole and saw that it was Sage's mother, Mia. "You've got to be kidding me," She muttered. Sucking in air, she unlocked the door and opened it.

"Who the hell are you?" were Mia's greeting words.

Astrid stared back at the bright skinned woman sporting a pound of makeup. She'd never seen her up close, but she was evidently beautiful. From the flashy gold jewelry, sleek, violet bodysuit and black, satin Prada heels, she presumed her to be a bit high maintenance. The violet Prada bag on her wrist also added to Astrid's assumptions.

"My name is Astrid,"

"Astrid?" Mia repeated unflattered. She wore an expression so rigid her face was sure to break in two. "I've never met you before."

Astrid forced a smile. "You're Sage's mom. I know you."

"You don't know shit," Mia cocked. Sucking her teeth, she shoved Astrid to the side and entered the house. The stench of alcohol trailed along with her.

Closing the door, Astrid did her best not to gag at the harsh aroma. "Uh, is there anything I can help you with?"

Mia faced her. "I should be the one asking you that. You got my child. You supposed to be Zane's new bitch? I warned his ass about having his hoes around my daughter."

Astrid bit her tongue in an effort not to verbally retaliate. She wanted to put the bold woman in her place, but she settled to leave that piece to Zane. "I'm his secretary," she stated.

"Hmmp. I bet you are. You're supposed to be Sage's new mother too, huh?" Mia cut her eyes. "You know, it really just hit me. I do know who you are."

Here we go, Astrid thought.

She braced herself. Living in Saxton all of this time without having a run in with a stranger who knew nothing about her? She wasn't sure how she managed to convince herself that she wouldn't. She was bound to run into at least one. She just didn't expect it to hit so close to home.

"You're the bitch who almost got my Donovan arrested," Mia disclosed.

"Excuse me?"

"Yes. My man Donovan. You got Zane to call the police the moment y'all found that bitch's body. He almost got found out because of you."

"Mia, what the hell are you talking about?"

Mia smirked arrogantly. "The fact that you're asking me that lets me know how Donovan has gotten as far as he has all of this time. You are one cloudy bitch. You should've stayed your weak ass in Daytona. Zane would've been locked away by now."

Astrid stared speechless at the ruthless woman. She could feel where this was going. Donovan was behind Layla's murder. As confused as she was in that moment, she had a feeling that wasn't the only foul thing he'd done. Fear gripped her at the numerous unknown possibilities. "Mia, I think you better leave."

"Or what?" Mia challenged, "You plan on calling Zane on me? Trust me, you won't make it that far. I swear, Donovan should've taken you out himself the moment Gabe's bipolar ass fucked up that night on the swanny. All that money my cousin Othello paid to have you. He's still in prison collecting dust over your bullshit confession."

Astrid felt her heart drop. She took a step away from Mia, and her back hit the front door.

Othello?

Mia's cousin?

He paid Donovan?

Suddenly it felt as if the room was closing in on her. Was she dreaming again? Maybe she'd fallen asleep in the porch chair in between reading Zora Neal Hurston and watching Sage, and now she was once again trapped inside of another one of her twilight zone nightmares?

"This is surprising to you?" Mia interrogated. "You're the reason why Gabe killed himself. He couldn't take the guilt of being an asset in helping the fat ballerina get set up. Bet money that Zane knew all along. Why do you think he feels so guilty? Shit, he should be on my side. It's your ass who convinced him to take Sage away from me..."

Gabe set me up?

Zane knew?

Astrid wasn't sure what to make of anything else Mia said. Somewhere after her claiming that Zane knew about what Donovan had done, she zoned out. She was back on the Swanny during her senior night. She was tied up. Drugged. Othello and the other stranger were arguing.

"I swear this is my last time doing this shit. Fuckin' brother would kill me."

"You wanna start this late in the game by giving a fuck just because you know her?"

"Just do your best and try not to be so damn rough. I need her in one piece unlike your other previous work."

Astrid remembered it all. The moment she wondered how Othello found her cabin after blacking out in the Parakeet bar. When she begged to be let go. When the stranger—Gabe, looked back at her with guilt in his eyes before leaving out of the cabin. As if he wanted to undo everything that was about to unfold in Astrid's life...

How could she have not known?

"I'm going to kill you for all its worth." Mia said vengefully.

Blinking, Astrid was brought back to the present. Her eyes fell on the gun pointed at her. Her heart pounded vigorously as Mia stared back at her with loathe in her eyes. The turning click of the gun as she cocked it erupted like an echo of loud metal.

Astrid closed her eyes.

The pain in her womb.

The ways of Daytona.

The death of Ariyah.

It'd all prepared her for this moment.

She was sure she would die from the cause of one of those events, but fate apparently had other plans.

It was the curdling scream of Sage that jilted her out of her attempt to surrender. Opening her eyes, Astrid turned her attention in the direction of the porch. "Sage..." she whispered.

"Astrid!" she screamed once again.

As fast as the wind itself, Astrid ran out of the front door's entry hall. She flinched at the ear-shattering shot Mia fired in her direction. The bullet went zooming inches above her head right before she turned the corner, leading her back out into the screened porch and into the backyard where a group of men completely surrounded it.

One of them, tall and menacing, held Sage in place as she tussled back and forth.

"No!" Astrid screamed. She attempted to run towards Sage but one of the guard men caught her and held her firmly in place as well. "Please! Let her go!" she begged.

Raising his hand, the man holding Sage snapped his fingers and motioned for one of the crewmen to come over and get her.

Sage fought furiously against the captives, but she was no match for their strength. Astrid watched in horror as she screamed while being carried away out of the backyard. Out of her sight.

"Please!" Astrid cried. "Bring her back! Take me!"

"Oh, baby," a familiar voice said from behind her. "We already plan on doing that."

The man holding Astrid ordered for her to calm down before unleashing her to the ground. Pain shot through her knees, but it was nothing like the reminiscing pain in her heart. It was as if she were reliving Aryiah being taken away from her all over again. Holding her stomach, she looked back at the house where Donovan stood in the porch's doorway.

"I'm pretty sure I got it from here." he informed the crewmen.

One by one, they all exited the yard except the one who ordered Sage to be taken away. He eyed Astrid closely as he walked over to whisper something to Donovan. The two of them exchanged words before shifting their attention back to her.

"Get up," the man ordered her gruffly.

Astrid heard him, but she'd suddenly forgotten how to walk. She forgot how to breathe. Everything inside of her was going on a whirlwind.

This isn't happening again. God this isn't happening.

"You gon make the boss repeat himself," Donovan barked. "Get your fucking ass up!" Slowly, Astrid Walking over to her, the man reached out to touch her face, but Astrid quickly turned her head. She closed her eyes tightly, tears streaming down her cheeks. She shuddered when she felt the man lean in and put his lips to her ear.

"Listen to me closely," he told her. "Keys Resort. The harbor. Boat 13. Underneath the bed. It's loaded. I got Sage. Z will handle Donovan."

Opening her eyes, Astrid released a rugged breath. She stared up at the man. Searched his eyes and saw the valuable explanation behind his words. This was a web inside of a set up.

"Yo, D! Tell your lady to try not to make too much of a mess!" the man barked over his shoulder without breaking eye contact with

Astrid. "The Saxton boys in blue are hell on us street cats, but they're even worse on our beloved lady counterparts!"

Donovan laughed menacingly. "Damn right!"

"Make a scene." the man muttered to Astrid.

Astrid accepted the invitation. She reasoned this situation could go either way. Either she was going to be proven a fool, or he was telling the truth. She chose to believe the latter.

As the man turned to walk away, Astrid began screaming and clawing at the back of his jacket like the helpless victim she was supposed to be. She cursed. Threw blows at his back. Cried more tears than she'd ever done since the news of her beloved Ariyah.

It was Mia firing off a warning shot into the air that prompted her to stop.

"Bitch, I suggest you figure out how you should act before I put a bullet in you right now instead of later!"

Indeed, Astrid stopped on command. She'd made her point. On his way out of the backyard gate, the man stole another look at her before disappearing.

"Do me a favor, baby," Donovan directed at Mia. "Handcuff her ass. Put her in the backseat and drive her down to the harbor. I got a few customers lined up and they're paying big money."

"Why are you doing this?" Astrid asked in a hollow tone.

Donovan stared back at her with minimal emotion. "You've always been trouble Astrid. You won't be that by the time I get done. I plan on killing Zane and raising Sage the way she should be raised; to do everything I tell her to do."

Anger went bolting through Astrid. "You're the one who's been hurting her."

"Why, Astrid, whatever do you mean?" he retorted sarcastically.

"You did to her what you paid Othello to do to me." Astrid said in a wounded tone. "You raped her. You're a fucking monster."

Donovan smirked. "I'll take that compliment."

The amount of rage that stirred through Astrid was uncanny. She shifted her attention back to Mia as she walked over still aiming the gun at her with handcuffs. She continued to cooperate. But silently, she couldn't wait to get her hands on her own weapon fast enough.

If fate would have it, Zane would have Donovan. But Mia—as a mother, Astrid determined, she was hers to put into the ground. pulled herself to her feet.

Black Russian Roulette
ZANE

Zane stood out on the Western Saxton bridge in awe. He stared at the fourteen-carat diamond ring embedded inside of a black velvet ring box. There was no way for him to form the emotions he felt. No woman had ever prompted him to go to such lengths.

Yet here he was.

Rehearsing over and over in his head how he would ask Astrid to marry him.

The playboy was long overdue in his actions. For the past two months, he hadn't been able to shake it. He was in love. The feeling rested on him like butterflies to a flower in the summertime.

He wasn't caught off guard by it. It was the desire to tie Astrid down that surprised him. It came the very night she suffered her attack. He witnessed the pain in her eyes. Prayed for her, and heard God clear as day. The urge to want to take care of Astrid came over him far stronger than the previous times. He'd tried to put it off, thinking maybe the feeling would drown itself. Thinking that it would tuck itself away back where it came from.

It didn't.

Now, here he was. Trying to figure out how to tell the woman he always wanted, loved, that he wanted to take care of her for a lifetime.

Slipping the box into his pocket, Zane stared out thoughtfully along the bridge. He closed his eyes. Shut out the noise of traffic, car horns and the city birds. He tuned his ears to the sound of the rushing waters beneath.

Let it go, he told himself. It's not your fault. Gabe was tired. He wanted to rest, and he got it.

"Well, little brother. Your big brother has finally decided to settle down," Zane spoke out loud.

"I got my Queen. You'd be proud to know that. I been hanging on to you for a while. Dreamin' about you. Guess it's time for me to let you go so I can be the father Sage needs. So, I can be the man Astrid needs..."

When the wind blew, Zane inhaled. Tears tugged at the gates of his eyes and streamed down into the nest of his beard. It was as if he could feel Gabe's hand rest on his shoulder. He could hear his laughter.

"I know little brother," he said. "I'm proud of you too. I never stopped being that. You wanted peace and you got it."

It was a few more minutes before Zane wiped away the tears from his eyes and gathered himself. At the same time, his cellphone rang. It was Serenity.

"Serenity, what's up, love? I'm on my way."

"Zane," Serenity said. It was the fragility of her voice that alerted him.

"What's wrong?"

"It's Sage and Astrid! They're gone!" She cried. "They're gone, Zane!"

"Say what?"

"They're missing! And your place is a mess! Like somebody came and trashed it! Zane you've got to get here quick!"

"Okay. I need you to go back to your car and wait. I'm going to call Donovan."

"Okay. I called Blaze. He's on the way too."

"Alright. Bet."

Hanging up, Zane called up Donovan, but he didn't answer. "Damn it, D! Come on!" He hissed. He called him again, but still there was no answer.

"Fuck!" Zane blurted to the sky. He could feel the harsh drumming of his heart through his chest. He sought to call Astrid but there was no answer from her either. "Come on, sweetheart," he muttered as he redialed her number again. He made his way across the street to his Ferrari.

"Pick up," he urged. "Just let me know you good."

Just as before, Astrid failed to answer. Zane muttered a few more foul words as he retrieved his keys to unlock his door. It was the ringing of his cellphone that halted him again.

"Ring," Zane answered. "Yo, we got a problem."

"Damn right we do," Ring confirmed. "Zane, listen, before you go off, Astrid is fine. She's with me down here at the harbor. I just got her off one of the boats. She's a little stunned right now. The policemen are here, but we've both been Ray Charles mode until otherwise."

"Boat? Policemen?" Zane repeated. "Ring, what the hell is going on?"

"Zane...Mia's dead. She tried to kill Astrid. It's too much to say over the phone but your boy Donovan ain't shit."

Zane rubbed at the top of his head as he processed the information relayed to him. "Did you just say Mia is dead?"

"Yes."

"Where's my daughter?"

"She's being brought to you..."

"Brought to me? Give Astrid the phone..."

There was a short pause on the line before Astrid came on.

"Zane," she spoke in a withered tone. "Astrid? Baby what's going on?"

"I'm so sorry," Astrid cried. "She didn't give me a choice. It's Donovan. It was him. It's been him the whole time..."

It was the sound of screeching tires that caught Zane's attention. Turning around, he was faced with four black cars surrounding him.

"The fuck?" He muttered as one of the drivers stepped out.

"Zane Keys," the man spoke. "That's you right?"

"Depends on who's asking?" Zane replied militantly.

"We got someone who belongs to you..." the man stated.

Zane took in the seriousness of the man's stance. "Astrid," he muttered, "I promise you, I'm going to come get you baby. But right now, I need you to give the phone back to Ring."

"Zane," Astrid spoke softly. "I love you..."

Zane's heart skipped a beat at the untimely confession. "I love you too, Queen."

"Yo, Zane?" Ring came back on.

"Ring, answer me this, are you a part of this shit?" He inquired in a hardened tone. "Zane, I'm far from being the one who's your enemy." Ring cleared.

"That's all I need to know."

Hanging up, Zane stared sternly back at the unknown man. He could tell from his defensive posture that this wasn't some friendly meetup. His presence reeked of havoc, and Zane knew, for whatever reason, Sage and Astrid were the bait at the center of it all.

"Whatever your beef is with me," Zane told him. "Just let my people go and we can handle this."

Looking him over, the man turned his attention to the car parked beside him. The driver's seat door opened, and another man of brilliant height and obvious dominance with broad shoulders exited. The rest of the men who occupied the other cars did the same.

"Langston?" Zane identified.

"Z," Langston greeted with a smirk. "Long time no see, ole' partner."

If this were some casual run-in, perhaps Zane would've been more appeased to greet one of his old street partners. But considering the matter at hand, he was in no mood for some formal reunion.

"The hell is this about?" Zane asked.

"Layla Brooks, ring a bell?"

The vision of Layla's body in the bathtub flashed in his memory.

"I take it from the look on your face that it does," Langston concluded.

"I didn't kill her. We had one night together. Whatever your connection is with her—"

"She's the estranged daughter of my boss. Binx." Langston informed him.

"Binx?"

"Yeah. And I know you didn't kill her. But you are associated with the person who did. I can't lie. Shit made you look guilty for a moment."

No one came to mind except Donovan. Zane grew even more livid at the thought. He'd warned him about doing work with the hot-blooded Italian dealer. Still, the mystery as to why he and Layla were associated plagued him.

"You're not that lost, I see," Langston carried on. "We're both aware that Donovan works for Binx. The boss started to go after him himself. But you know how it is when you keep your ears to the streets. You find out shit. Everything comes full circle. I managed to talk Binx into letting you handle that."

"Langston, we both know I've been done with this lifestyle for a while now. Secondly, I've never been one to cross family."

Langston nodded before walking over to the backseat of his SUV and opened the door.

"Come on, lil' mama. It's okay."

Zane saw his daughter's shoes hit the asphalt before her face appeared from around the car door.

"Daddy!" Sage shrieked. Running over to him, she wrapped her arms securely around her father.

"Sage..." Zane embraced her tightly. "It's okay baby. I'm here. I've got you."

"He hurt me, daddy," Sage cried furiously. Zane glared at Langston.

"Nah, Z." Langston raised his hands in defense. "She ain't talkin' about me."

Pulling back, Zane stared down at Sage.

"Please don't hate me!" She begged. "I wanted to tell you, but he threatened to hurt you!"

Zane cupped his daughter's face in his hands. "Sage, who hurt you? Tell me!"

Sage sniffled, "Donovan," she replied.

Zane felt his heart crush in two. It was as if the world set itself on top of him. It was the same feeling he encountered the night Gabe ended it all. The difference is that it was also accompanied with rage.

"You got a foul ass motherfucka around you, Z." Langston said. "Real foul. I can assure you, Astrid is taken care of. But I just need to know if we got a deal? If so, I'll fill you in on every damn thing I know."

∽

Zane dropped his cigar onto the asphalt just as he saw Donovan pull into one of the parking lots in front of the Cigar Palace. He released the leftover smoke from his lips. Adjusted his leather jacket to ensure the gun he had tucked into the back hold of his jeans was hidden.

Closing his eyes, he silently asked God to forgive him for the sin he was about to commit.

For the last few hours up until the sun rested over the city of

Saxton, Zane wrestled with himself. Langston and Ring both filled him in on the calculating events committed by the man he called friend since adolescence.

Ring was missing in action for one sole reason: he'd been working undercover for Binx. Per request of both him, and Langston, Ring followed Donovan around for the last six weeks until all of the dots began to connect. Until things that weren't expected to be revealed.

Donovan was a snake.

"I owed Binx a favor from some years back." Ring revealed, *"I was going through some illegal financial issues. Let's just say I owe him my life. Imagine my surprise when Binx contacts me because he thinks he has someone foul working in his camp. Shit like his valuables, his money coming up missing, and the culprit is Donovan..."*

"Layla was collateral," Langston uncovered. *"But she was the wrong collateral."*

Wrong collateral. Layla was exactly that. And Donovan was oblivious to it all. Greed blinded him long ago.

He'd gotten away with remaining a hidden piece in Astrid's rape. Guilting Gabe into suicide. Forming a romantic alliance with Mia. Stealing Sage's innocence. Donovan had gotten away with so much for so long that he became convinced he could commit evil harm without error.

For a while, he was satisfied with the things Zane didn't know. He did well at making money. But somewhere along the way, his jealousy shifted to envy. It was around the time Zane quit the streets and became far too successful.

Too many people began to know him. Too much money followed him. And most of all, even more women flocked to him.

"Unbeknownst to most people, I'm a master at technology," Ring disclosed to Zane. *"From an illegal standpoint, that is. I managed to*

tap into Donovan's cell. The conversations he and Mia have shared, Z. You owe that motherfucka a nightmare."

Donovan knew nothing about Binx being Layla's father. Or that he and his daughter hadn't spoken in years. He didn't know that while the two had bad blood, nonetheless, they were still blood and Binx was set on having his head.

Donovan had secretly grown so power hungry that he killed Layla with the intent to get Zane locked away. But when that didn't work, the next plan was to have him assassinated. He would create a fake will stating that Zane left him everything. He would even go so far as to contact the Ryan brothers and discuss future business endeavors with them. Afterall, he'd been the one to lead the white men to Zane in the first place.

When all hell was done breaking loose, and Zane and Astrid were in the ground, Donovan would marry Mia, take her and Sage, and move out of the state with the money he'd stolen from Binx. He would have wealth from both worlds, both honest and dishonest all at once.

The plan was genius to him, but Donovan made the mistake of letting the most loyal person to Binx see his hand, Langston. In return, Langston would get someone in Donovan's circle who was far more loyal to Zane to snake him back, Ring.

"You're supposed to be dead right now," Langston stated. "And your daughter was supposed to see it happen..."

The conversation with Langston and Ring played in Zane's mind. He wrestled with the fact that he could call Detective's Reid and Grant and put them up on game. Or he could choose to handle things himself.

He chose the latter.

Opening his eyes, Zane made his way across the street and into the palace. He overlooked the friendly smiles and head nods of acknowledgements from the bartenders, happy hour locals and smokers. A few waiters and waitresses spoke to him, but their greetings went unheard as well. He searched over the mildly crowded establishment, and spotted Donovan in the corner tucked between two women.

He was so wrapped into his promiscuous company that he didn't notice Zane at first. When he did, he ceased mid conversation. His expression, bewildered. "Z..." he said, the tone of his voice of a man who was caught off guard.

"Yo, I've been trying to get a hold of you for the last three hours."

"Bet?" Donovan replied. He stared up at Zane for a moment then stood. He put on the illusion of urgency by reaching into his pocket for his phone. "I didn't get a call from you."

"I called you more than three times."

"Nah, bruh. You didn't. At least not from my end."

"Doesn't look like you would've heard it," Zane said casually.

The halfway amused chuckle that erupted from Donovan's throat was fraudulent. "Right," he replied. "I guess that's on me. Binx had me doing drops all the way over in Velvet County today." He exclaimed. "Two hours out. Shit was strenuous. You know I couldn't wait to get back to the goods."

Zane didn't respond to Donovan's bogus rambling. He just stared back at him. Unmoved. Unimpressed. His mind drifted off to the mystery of how he'd missed it all before pulling himself back.

Nervously, Donovan scratched at the back of his head and then tugged at his shirt collar. "Uh, yeah." he muttered. "But you know I gotchu. Have a seat, brother."

Sitting, Zane forced himself to swallow the venom that built up in his throat at the usage of the word brother. Just how much of a brother could he have been to the man before him for him to cross the line to this magnitude? He watched calmly as Donovan dismissed the women and reclaimed his seat.

"I've been looking for you all day," Zane reiterated. "Some mad shit has gone down. I think you were right about Astrid."

Scratching at the back of his head again, Donovan raised an eyebrow. "Oh yeah? What makes you say that?"

"I haven't wanted to acknowledge it for a while, but she's been distant. This afternoon, I called her to check on Sage, and she didn't pick up. So, I got Serenity to go by my place and check. She calls me, frantic as hell. Talking about my entire place has been vandalized, and both Astrid and Sage are missing."

"You're serious?"

"Hell yeah. And you won't believe what happened after that. I'm driving down the Western Bridge on the way to my house, and the next thing I know, four black cars came out of nowhere and started chasing me. I managed to get away, but I think she set that up too. It's why I've been blowing you up. Nigga been hidin' out from this shit. I tried calling Serenity back since our last phone call, but she hasn't been answering. I think something's gone wrong in her end too."

"Emmp," Donovan grunted.

"That's all you got to say?"

"What?" Donovan's voice cracked. "Nah. I mean…I," Donovan cleared his throat. "Look, Z. I tried to tell you. That bitch ain't shit. People don't change that much."

"Yeah, you did," Zane replied melancholy. "Blaze is going to kill me if something's happened to his wife. I just thought I had this shit right this time."

"I didn't wanna say this. But earlier today, when I was at the resort, Astrid tried to make a move on me. Asking me if I would come and see her later after she got home from watching Sage."

"What?"

"Hell yeah," Donovan carried on. "Basic broad, man. But you wanted to play save a hoe."

"Damn, I fucked up."

When one of the waitresses approached their table inquiring if they would like something to drink, Donovan couldn't seem to order something harsh over the rocks fast enough.

"Okay, coming right up," the waitress replied. "Anything for you, Mr. Keys?"

Zane looked up at the brown skinned, slim framed woman. "No thank you, Ashley. Do yourself a favor, when you're done preparing Mr. Price's drink, go home."

The waitress stared back at him a bit confused. "I'm sorry. Did I do something wrong?"

Zane smiled back at her reassuringly. "Of course not. You'll still get paid for your scheduled hours. And pass the word on to the rest of the crew. We're closing early tonight. Everyone is free to go. No one will be docked."

The waitress grinned widely. "Yes sir," she replied walking away.

"You're sending all of your workers home?" Donovan asked.

"Hell yeah. We gotta come up with a master plan, D. That means we can't risk the possibility of being heard."

Donovan peered around the cigar palace. His attention floated towards the entrance door as he watched customers begin to be escorted out, the women he was entertaining included. He tugged uncomfortably at his shirt collar.

"Were you expecting somebody?" Zane asked him.

Donovan looked back at him. "Nah," he mumbled.

"Good. We don't need any distractions. I'm bugged out enough. I swear, I'm probably being watched right now."

Neither of the men spoke until the waitress came back to the table and placed Donovan's drink down in front of him. In the meantime, the cigar palace emptied out and fear was heavily poured in.

In all of his years, Zane had never seen a man more displaced. Donovan was a hard one. There was nothing that seemed to ever dislodge him. It was a trait Zane admired up until earlier that day. The man he'd called friend was an enemy who mirrored putrid intimidation. So much so that while he'd waited for the waitress to return with his drink, he'd excused himself to supposedly take a phone call from Binx only to return even more disgruntled.

"I'm not trying to get you caught up in me and Astrid's shit, alright?" Zane made it clear. "I know this one's on me. But considering that you got more pull in the streets, I thought maybe you could get some eyes out for me."

Donovan took a long sip from his drink and set it down on the table. Unconsciously, he was tapping one of his shoes along the floor eagerly. "Uh, that would mean you want war, Z," he said.

"You mean to tell me you're that furious with Astrid all of a sudden?"

"You're saying I'm going too far?" Zane inquired solemnly.

"I'm sayin' your head's been in the clouds. You should sleep on it before we plan anything. Give yourself until tomorrow morning. If you want, I can go look for Sage..."

Zane felt the heat of his rage further rise to the surface at the horrid proposition. "Damn," he muttered, continuing with his act. He rubbed at his beard as if he were focused on brainstorming. "I guess you're right,"

"Of course."

"Detectives' have already been on my ass. But let me ask you a question," Zane said. "How much money do you think it'll take to stop them from trying to frame me for Layla's death?" Donovan tapped his shoe even harder. "

"The hell you talking about, Z? They already know you didn't do it."

Zane shook his head. "Let me be more specific. How much money should I pay them to make this whole thing go away? Should it be the same amount Othello paid my brother to rape Astrid? Or should I go all out and give them what you planned on putting in my will?"

Donovan paused in the anxious act of tapping his shoe along the floor. He stared back at Zane, his eyes now mirroring a man who was connecting the dots in what was just said to him.

"What should I do, Mr. Price?" Zane said in a hardened tone. "Your beloved brother, Z, is lost as fuck..."

Donovan couldn't seem to leap up from his chair fast enough towards the exit doors. With all his strength, he did his best to break them down.

Meanwhile, Zane remained unmoved. He watched Donovan try his best to escape. He watched him curse the air when he realized his attempt was in vain and took off towards the back of the palace. It wasn't long before he reappeared back out into the open floor, his expression haunted at what he'd seen.

"Shit! The fuck did you do to Mia?" Donovan inquired short winded. Perspiration drained from his forehead and streamed down his face as if he'd taken a swim into the same unsettled waters that streamed along the underpass of the Western bridge as Gabe did. "Who the fuck put her body at the back door?"

Zane stood. "You'll have to take that up with my future wife," he told him. "Then again, you won't be here to do that."

When Donovan went over to the exit doors and attempted to break them down again, he grew even more furious than the last time that they wouldn't give way. "Fuck!" he barked.

"They're locked," Zane informed him. "All of the doors are locked. With chains from the outside to be exact."

Breathing hard, Donovan turned around to face him.

"What? You're going to kill me now motherfucka!"

"You're already dead, D." Zane replied, reaching for his gun out of the back hold of his pants. "I'm just catching you up." Aiming his gun at Donovan, Zane fired off two rounds.

"Ahhhh!!!" Donovan growled in agony. He dropped helplessly to the floor. The two bullets pierced both sides of his shoulders, ruthlessly tearing through his shoulder blades. "I got backup, nigga!" he winced.

"Who? Binx? Langston? The crewmen?" Zane named them off one by one. "That's your backup?"

Donovan struggled to answer. He groaned while trying to slide along the floor away from Zane.

"I swear, they're…going to…fuck you up! You and that bitch!"

Walking over to the bar, Zane picked up one of the leftover empty beer bottles and broke it over the edge of the counter. Approaching Donovan, he stood over him. "I'm going to give you a choice. Either I end you, or Binx does."

"The fuck…is you talkin'…about? I got eyes…on you. Your ass…is dead too."

"You're not answering the question. So let me further break this down in a way for you to understand. You bought yourself a burial plot when you killed Layla considering she's the daughter of Binx. But violating my daughter, playing on my twin brother's emotional intelligence, stealing pieces of the woman I've always loved to the point where it haunted her for years, that shit granted your ass a funeral…"

When Donovan parted his lips to speak again, Zane fired off another round into his left knee.

"Ahhhhh, shit!" he howled in agony once more.

Placing the safety back on, Zane tucked the gun back into the hold of his jeans. He crouched down over Donovan. "This is the part of myself that I locked away," he said. "You wanted to be a heartless nigga? I'll make you one."

Positioning the broken bottle in the center of Donovan's chest, Zane pressed the sharp, pointed glass into his flesh hard enough to puncture skin. Hard enough to break through cartilage and bone and eventually pierced his heart.

Donovan's screams of torture could be heard for miles outside of the Cigar Palace, but no one was coming to save him. He fought to hold on just as Astrid had that night on the Swanny. Just as Gabe had on top of the Western Bridge. Just as Sage was still doing.

It was the lethal thrust and twist of the broken glass bottle lodged into his chest that stole the last breath from him. Zane watched life slip from Donovan's eyes until there was nothing there but hollowness.

Standing to his feet, he backed away from the dead body. He fought the tears that burned at the corners of his eyes. Wiped at the perspiration that drained from the pores of his face. Reaching into his pocket, he retrieved his cell phone and dialed Langston.

"What's up, boss man?" Langston answered.

"It's done," Zane muttered.

"Bet. We'll unlock the chains." Langston informed him. "As far as Mia and Donovan's bodies, we got that. Go home."

Ending the phone call, Zane made his way over to the exit doors and walked out. As soon as he did, he spotted Astrid standing alongside one of the crewmen across the street.

The two of them, both battered in spirit, made their way over to each other.

"Hey, King." Astrid greeted softly.

"Hey, ballerina," Zane greeted back huskily.

Astrid smiled weakly at him. She wanted to say more, but her emotions wouldn't let her. Instead, she closed in the space between them by wrapping her arms around Zane.

"It's okay," he assured her. He pressed his lips to her neck and placed a kiss there. "I've got you."

"I've got you too," Astrid told him.

Home Is Where the Heart Has Always Been

SIX MONTHS LATER

"Alright, alright, my lovebird listeners. We're going to slow it down a bit on this beautiful Saturday night for the lovers, an old school throwback from Mary J Blige. If you have someone nearby that you love, grab them close and hold on. Silk Jams, 103.6."

Astrid gripped her hands along the holding rail of the yacht. She closed her eyes and felt the smooth breeze of the night air caress her skin. The sun hadn't long ago set over the horizon, giving the sky a brownish, orange peak. She and her husband sailed along the waters of Mater Bay planted in the heart of Charmington City. The smooth tunes of Mary J Blige's "I'm In Love" blaring from the radio caressed both her heart and spirit. There was no way around it. She was as free as she'd ever been in her entire life.

"I love seeing you this way..." the baritone voice tickled her ears like silk.

"What way?"

"The way you're supposed to be. Free."

A delicate smile curved Astrid's lips. Turning around, she faced Zane in time to catch him staring back at her in the most enticing way. "You make me feel that way," she told him.

Zane smiled, and Astrid felt herself go weak. What was it? She still didn't know. No man had ever made her feel warm by doing such a simple gesture. "You really shouldn't smile like that at me," she told him.

"Hmmp," Zane blushed. He rubbed at his beard as his eyes traveled down to the center of Astrid's stomach where the long scar was imprinted on her skin. Reaching out, he grazed his thumb over it. "You're healing nicely. I'll be sure to send Dr. Rucker my regards when we touch back down in Sax."

"Mhmmm. And I'm going to pay you back every cent."

"Now, we both know that's bogus, baby. You wanna pay me back," Zane tugged her into his embrace, "Love me forever," he told her. "Keep having my back, and I'm going to have your front. Always." He raised her hand and kissed the finger that graced the fourteen-carat diamond ring. "You can start by letting me make love to you again..."

"Lead the way, King."

Zane laughed huskily as he began guiding her in the direction of the cabin, but halfway there, Astrid paused her footsteps. She shifted her attention back to the radio propped on the seat.

Zane encircled his arms around her waist. "What's wrong, sweetheart?" he asked.

Astrid placed her fingers gently to his lips. "Listen..."

It was the music. It stopped. The radio spokesman cut in with an announcement about an important news development before he was then interrupted with a local news reporter.

"Local authorities of Daytona County have finally caught and arrested Marvin Foreman, also known as the notorious drug dealer,

Daytona. Authorities say he was spotted by a customer at a gas station just miles outside of Saxton city limits dressed in a black hoodie, and sweats. He is the last one in the case of the Little Angels daycare shooting where seven toddlers and five adults were sadly killed a year ago. According to the residents of Daytona, they are as relieved as the authorities. We've also been informed that Mr. Foreman has no bond..."

Zane embraced Astrid tightly against him. He pressed his lips to her ear. "I told you. God didn't forget about you."

Astrid blinked away the tears fighting to spill from her eyes and looked up at Zane. She searched his eyes and saw exactly that. She saw God in him. She saw everything peaceful. Just. Right. She saw life, and everything fruitful in it. She saw love. Forgiveness. She saw the beautiful things of a world she'd yet to fully explore.

Cupping his bearded face in her hands, she pressed her lips to his in a kiss so deep that she was sure to lose her balance. As usual, Zane was steps ahead of her. He scooped her up into an embrace, leaving her the free will to wrap her legs securely around his waist.

"I've got something to show you, Mrs. Keys," Zane whispered to her.

He carefully carried her down to the cabin where he laid her out on the bed and committed to faithfully removing her soft, pink, two-piece bathing suit piece by piece. He took in the delicateness of her face, the beautiful fullness of her breasts. She'd cut her locs down low some weeks ago out of impulse, and the beauty move brought out the erotic shape of her eyes.

"Tell me what you want," Zane muttered to her seductively.

Leaning her head to the side, Astrid nibbled at her lower lip. "I want you to taste me," she told Zane. "But first, I want you to take off your clothes."

Zane smirked sexily. "You most definitely can have that."

Taking a step back, Zane removed his shirt revealing his brown, husky chest. He removed his khaki sail shorts down to his underwear. The engorged flesh between his full thighs pressed heavily along the cotton fabric.

Clamping her legs together, Astrid inhaled at the sight. The first night they made love, she requested Zane take it extra slow with her. But over the timeframe of their honeymoon out on the Mater Bay, she grew accustomed to his length to the point of becoming overly excited. She'd encountered men of hefty size, but none of them knew how to use it. None of them knew how, or even cared to know how to please her like Zane. In that moment, she fought to contain the throbbing between her thighs. Her struggle was obvious to the big man before her, and he didn't dare let up.

Slowly, Zane removed his underwear, exposing the length of his shaft.

Astrid swallowed hard as she took in the mouthwatering sight of the man who was now her husband of eight days. The tattoos that decorated his body. The bulkiness of his frame. He was everything she didn't know she needed. Her eyelashes fluttered as he walked over to her and dropped down to his knees.

"Don't fight me, Mrs. Keys," Zane told her playfully as he gently pried her thighs apart. "You'll only make it harder for yourself."

Astrid smiled erotically. She laid back on the soft bed beneath her and did her best to prepare for the mind trap to come. There wasn't enough time in the world for that.

Like a man dying of thirst, Zane gripped her thighs and brought her to the edge of the bed. Spreading her, he took a deep dive into her cave, hungrily devouring her. He fluttered his tongue along the delicate parts of her folds. Sucked at the center of her beautiful pearl in a way that made her back arch upwards.

Helpless, Astrid sunk into glorious depths. With her eyes closed, she drifted into the deep end of nowhere, yet somewhere beautiful all at once. She fought and was stricken down over and over. Her cries of ecstasy set off alarms on the inside of Zane, causing his already hard shaft to become even more rigid.

When Astrid began to shake, Zane braced himself to catch all of her. He held her securely in place as she shivered, bucked. Balled her hands into the bedcovers and did her best to hold onto herself while floating in orbit. Like a volcano, she erupted onto his taste buds until there was nothing left.

When she was done, Zane cleaned her up with the tantalizing brushing of his tongue along her valley. He licked her clean before trailing wet streaks along her inner thighs all the way up to her ankles and toes.

Astrid giggled at the ticklish feeling.

Reaching out to cup his face between her hands, she tugged Zane upwards to her. Prompting him to take her mouth captive just as he had before. She sucked at his tongue in a way that caused his shaft to twitch.

"Emmm, Astrid," Zane moaned in between kisses. Gripping his hand around her neck, he looked her in the eyes. "Ride me," he told her huskily.

Astrid inhaled sharply at her husband's command. "Yes," she replied, breathlessly.

Positioning himself on the bed, Zane took in his wife's plush honey shaded frame as she straddled him. She positioned herself over him, and inch by inch, slid down his swollen length.

"That's it, baby." He affirmed. He gripped her hips, and slightly raised his up to meet her, thrusting himself further into her cave.

Astrid gasped as she felt herself open up to him. He filled up every corner of her. She placed her hands palms flat on his chest for balance and began rocking her hips back and forth. She started off slow, an erotic rhythm, strategically bringing Zane into the heated ring of ecstasy.

"Work that shit for me, baby." Zane moaned. He gripped his

hands over her breasts. Teased at the hardness of her nipples between the padding of his fingers.

"Emmmm," Astrid cried. She threw her head back at the feel of his hands. Like the motion of the yacht, she rowed her hips over the continuous waves of hot thrusts.

When she picked up her speed, Zane raised his hips again, thrusting up and down. The high-pitched throaty moans that drifted from Astrid's lips informed him that he was hitting the right spots just as she was doing for him. He grazed his thumb along the fullness of her lips before sliding it into her mouth, giving her free reign to suckle it.

The move was mind blowing. The way she gyrated her hips while sucking his fingers.

The feeling of love making for them both was magic. A never-ending sensation from their bodies coming together to fill up spaces inside of one another.

Just when Zane felt himself coming to his peak, he swiftly gripped Astrid's waist and positioned her on her back where he drove the rest of the way. Passionately, he rocked his hips between her thighs. In and out. In and out. He drove himself into her. Locked eyes with her to witness her walls tumbling down.

"Ohhh, Zane," Astrid groaned. "Please...." she cried.

Picking up speed, Zane braced himself to be thrown over the bridge of orgasm as well. He drove them both to the brink until the room around them seemed to resemble stars falling out of the sky. Until the sound of release fell from their lips in unison, and the only thing there was left for them to fall into was a peaceful sleep.

Some time, during the middle of the night, Astrid found herself tossing and turning enough to wake Zane. She wasn't troubled, but her spirit was restless.

"You okay?" he asked her.

With her head resting on his chest, Astrid traced invisible shapes there. "I think it's time for me to talk to my family," she revealed.

"As in face to face?"

"Yes."

Tugging her chin up to look at him, Zane took in the sincerity of her eyes. "Are you sure?"

Astrid nodded.

"When?"

"Tomorrow, when we get back to the harbor?" she suggested.

Zane stroked her cheek. "Okay, sweetheart," he said. "Whatever, you want."

"What if they don't want to see me anymore," Astrid confided in Zane as they sat in the car across the street from the medium-sized cottage. "I haven't been receptive."

"You had valid reasons, baby. But that won't be the case today." he assured her.

"How can you say that?"

Zane wiped at the tears that fell from his wife's eyes. "Let's just say I have a feeling," he told her.

Grabbing his hand, Astrid stared across the street at the beautiful cottage. Her grandparents always did have a way with appearance on things. Their gardening was one. The white orchids that grew along the edge of the house helped set off the rest of the green shrubbery surroundings. Aside from the giant oak tree firmly planted in the center of the yard, flowerpots hung from the roof. Two life sized statues graced the lawn. There was a cobblestoned pathway that led up to three steps connecting to a porch deck.

"Nothing has changed much," Astrid remarked warmly.

"You got this," Zane told her. "I'll be right here."

Astrid smiled at the reassurance of her husband's words. Leaning in to kiss him, she grazed her nose along his before exiting out of the car.

Taking a deep breath, Astrid made her way across the street. Walking along the cobblestone struck up a dozen memories before she could even reach the front door. Once she did, she raised her hand and gave a few light knocks. She took in the muffled sound of music playing, and familiar laughter.

Trina? She thought. *Sky?*

"You gotta knock harder than that baby!" Zane blurted.

Turning to look back at him, Astrid frowned as he smiled broadly. She didn't waver from his advice.

Raising her hand again, Astrid knocked even harder that time. She listened in as the music was lowered and replaced with the sound of footsteps getting closer to the door. Voices followed, and to her surprise, it was her sister Trina.

Taking a step back, Astrid's heartbeat erratically at the sound of the lock on the door being undone before it parted open, and she was face to face with her sister.

"Oh my God!" Trina gasped. "Astrid?"

"Hey..." she greeted, barely audible.

"Oh, baby sister!" Trina raved excitedly as she wrapped her arms around Astrid.

Astrid immediately broke down. She promised herself that she would be stronger, but her emotions had other plans. "I'm sorry," she whispered.

"No," Trina replied, pulling away from her. "You have nothing to apologize for."

"Trina!" Sky's voice erupted before she came into view. "Is she..."

Seeing her oldest sister Sky was like staring into the eyes of her mother. But as much of a mess as Astrid was at the sight of Trina, Sky became an even bigger mess at seeing her.

"Astrid..." Sky moaned. "My beautiful, Astrid."

Just as Trina had done, Sky wrapped her arms around her little sister's neck and cried hard. She cried so hard she developed hiccups. "Damn it," she fussed, stomping her feet along the porch.

"Look what you made me do!" Sky cupped Astrid's face. "Don't you dare go away that long again you hear me?"

Astrid nodded. "Okay, I promise."

The sisters continued to hug. But just when Astrid thought she'd gathered herself enough, her grandparents appeared.

"Will you two broads move out of our way!" Darina chastised before coming into view.

It was impossible for Astrid to contain herself at the sight of her grandparents. Time had aged them, but not harshly. Instead, grace and good eating had been on their side. They resembled a couple whose years on earth were kind to them.

"My baby is home," Darina marveled, her eyes glistening with tears.

"We missed you, baby girl," Abraham cosigned sweetly. "Welcome home!"

Both of them took turns greeting their granddaughter. They squeezed Astrid so hard she was sure her bones would break, and the feeling was a glorious one for her.

Astrid wasn't sure what made her cry more, her grandparents embrace, or the signature aroma of her grandfather's oven roast floating from the inside. Whichever one, she embraced it all.

"I'm so sorry, baby," Darina apologized to her. "We should've done better by you. Can you forgive us?"

Astrid smiled hard enough for her cheeks to hurt as fresh tears went streaming down her cheeks. "Of course, mama."

"Good!" Darina grinned. "I was hoping that husband of yours wasn't bluffin' me."

"Huh?"

"Zane called us late last night," Abraham told her. "Some time before the sun even got itself started. He said you were comin'. We were prepared for you. I stayed up all night cookin'"

"Uh-huh, and from the looks of you, you could use about four plates!" Darina exclaimed.

"Now, go get that husband of yours and you two get in here!"

Wiping her tears, Astrid turned to go get Zane, but he was already making his way through the cobblestones. Walking down to meet him, she pressed up on her tiptoes and flung her arms snuggly around him. "Thank you," she whispered.

"You're welcome, ballerina," Zane replied, warmly.

Meet the Author

Born and raised in a quiet neighborhood of Tallahassee, Florida, Shandra Ward has always had a love for books and writing. At the age of nine, she found solace in being a bookworm and later began creating colorful stories to accommodate the characters in her head. During her preteen years, Ward started out writing poems and short plays but it wasn't until she was fifteen after receiving a heartfelt piece of literature from a close friend, that she began taking her gift of writing seriously by transforming her plays into actual stories. Ward's favorite genres derive from a variety of fiction such as Romance, Fantasy, Drama, Urban-Lit, Horror, Mystery, and Christian Fiction as she never believed in limiting herself in the quest of gaining knowledge through the literary lenses of other authors.

Connect With Shandra Ward
facebook.com/AuthorShandraWard
instagram.com/authorshandraward

Made in the USA
Middletown, DE
14 May 2024

54225668R00106